Escape
with a
Hot
SEAL

HOT SEALS

Cat Johnson

CHAPTER ONE

"Ginny."

Virginia Starr tore herself away from staring at the worried face of the woman dressed in white reflected back at her in the wall mirror. She turned to look at her best friend. "Yeah?"

With two fingers Molly rolled the single pearl on the gold necklace, a gift from Ginny that morning.

"I think we might have to face the fact that just maybe he could not be coming."

Her maid of honor had used a whole lot of words to dance around what she'd really wanted to say. What could have been expressed with one short sentence had Molly been less concerned about sparing her feelings. *Left at the altar.*

Or, even simpler, one word—*jilted.*

It didn't matter what Molly thought. Ginny knew better.

She shook her head. "He said he'd be here, so he'll be here."

Molly's silence as she drew in a deep breath

spoke more than any words could have.

Turning back toward the dressing table, Ginny reached out and ran one fingertip over the delicate, crepe-like petals of one pink peony.

The peonies were interspersed with pale peach roses and white ranunculus, hand-tied with a sky blue satin ribbon. Simple but beautiful. All she'd dreamed of and everything she'd wanted for the day she publicly became Mrs. Thomas Grande.

Except in her dreams the groom wasn't MIA.

That term—missing in action—hit a little too close to home considering what Thom did for a living.

She pushed that thought aside. She didn't have to worry. For this week at least he wasn't away on some danger-filled, super secret mission . . . or was he?

Her eyes widened at the thought. Could he be? Wouldn't he tell her if he'd been called in?

She couldn't let the doubts creep in. She had to trust the man she loved. The man she'd be joined with in front of friends and family in the eyes of God—if Thom ever got his butt to the church.

A light knock sent Molly diving for the door. Breath catching in her chest, Ginny turned in time to see her parents peering into the doorway.

"How's she doing?" Ginny's mother cringed as she asked Molly the question.

Great. Now they were speaking about her like she wasn't in the room.

Scowling, Ginny answered, "I'm fine. He'll be here."

God, how she hoped he'd get there.

"I'm glad we didn't book that catering hall with the non-refundable deposit," her father said, low, but loud enough Ginny had heard it just fine.

"Mm, hm," her mother agreed, also softly, but also loud enough for her to hear.

Ginny clenched her jaw at the turn the discussion had taken. It wasn't as if she had ever wanted the catering hall to begin with.

She had told them not to book the hall that her mother had wanted. That the backyard at the house would be fine. More practical given their circumstances.

Molly glanced at her and then back to Ginny's parents. "We still have a little time."

The silence of unspoken disagreement was, once again, deafening.

Ginny closed her eyes and wondered—not for the first time—why she'd chosen to have this church ceremony and reception for close friends and family at all. Why she and Thom hadn't just eloped and left it at that.

Then she opened her eyes and caught a glimpse of herself in the mirror and she remembered why she'd put herself through this unnecessary stress.

She loved her dress, even if it was simple and off a department store rack because they hadn't had time for anything else.

And she loved the bouquet she'd made herself with flowers she'd bought at the florist. And the dozens of little white cup cakes, decorated with candied violets, that Thom's mother had baked for them in lieu of a traditional wedding cake. And the white lights—actually her parents' Christmas lights repurposed—strung in the trees in the backyard making her childhood home in Stamford look like a twinkling fairyland. And the hydrangeas—picked from bushes in that same backyard—displayed in mason jars and set out on the folding tables they'd borrowed from the local VFW.

She even loved the invitations she'd designed herself, the ones she had printed out on beautiful card stock she'd found at the local office supply store to save time.

Casual and inexpensive, but somehow perfect, this wedding was something she was proud of. It was all the things she and Thom had agreed it needed to be just in case he got yanked back to his base in Virginia for a mission and they had to reschedule.

But he hadn't been called back. He wasn't somewhere in the Middle East or where ever. He was in Pennsylvania, for goodness sake, at a hunting cabin with two of the guys from his team. He'd said they'd be home last night, but she hadn't heard from him. And his parents said he hadn't come back to their place in Massachusetts.

So where was he?

Could he have changed his mind about being married?

Fighting down the doubt, Ginny dared to look at the time on her cell phone. Five minutes to ten.

The ceremony was scheduled to start at ten. Glancing at the doorway again, she saw a new arrival had joined the group. The pastor.

The look of concern on the older man's face mirrored that of everyone else in the room.

"When's that baptism start?" she asked, already knowing the answer but hoping for a miracle. They were in church, after all. It was a good place for one.

"Eleven-thirty," he answered.

Ginny nodded, accepting the reality of what that meant.

They'd gone into this knowing he'd squeezed them into the schedule last minute. That it would have to be a short ceremony that started and ended on time.

Of course, weeks ago when she'd chosen this date she'd assumed if they'd have to cancel she'd have some advance notice. A week. A day even.

Certainly *not* five minutes.

Drawing in a bracing breath, Ginny somehow found strength she didn't know she had.

Or maybe it was detachment rather than strength, because this day was beginning to feel like it was happening to someone else and she was just an outside observer watching it unfold.

She smoothed the bodice of the white eyelet halter dress she'd bought on a summer clearance sale in spite of Molly's protests. Ginny stood straight and tall, rising to her full height—all five-foot-five inches of it, including her heels.

Taking one step toward the door she said, "I'll tell the guests."

CHAPTER TWO

Two Months Ago

The ring box in the cargo pocket of Thom Grande's tactical pants pressed against his leg. The hard square shape of the jewelers box served as a constant reminder as to why his chest felt tight and his gut twisted.

Not that he needed the reminder. There was no way he could forget what he'd decided to do.

He hadn't stopped second guessing the idea since the moment the crazy notion had crossed his mind. He certainly hadn't forgotten since he'd made the final payment when he'd picked up the ring this morning.

Sweating in spite of the A/C blowing on high in the chilled theater filled with SEALs, Thom plucked the neck of his T-shirt away from his skin.

How the hell long was this briefing going to last?

He blew out a huff and flopped against the padded back of the seat.

If attendance at this thing weren't required he'd totally—a boot stomped down on top of Thom's foot, cutting off that thought and focusing all his attention on the source of the attack.

"Ow." Frowning, Thom swiveled to glare at his teammate Brody Cassidy. He whispered, "What the hell? What's wrong with you?"

"Me?" Brody opened his eyes wide in a pointed stare. "You're the one who's been tapping your damn foot on the floor like a jackhammer for the past half hour. What's wrong with you?"

Brody was usually a pretty laid back type of guy, but something had obviously annoyed him today. Apparently—judging by the assault on his foot— that something had been Thom.

He hadn't even realized he'd been tapping his foot but he believed Brody. The man had no reason to lie and Thom certainly was distracted enough to have been doing what Brody had accused him of.

"Sorry." Thom drew in a breath. "I guess I'm a little antsy."

Brody let out a snort. "No shit."

Thom supposed that between his fidgeting in his seat and the racket his boot must have been making on the floor, his agitation was pretty obvious to Brody and anyone else seated nearby.

"So what's wrong? Ain't none of us wants to sit here all damn day for this briefing, but nobody else is crawling out of their skin about it like you are," Brody pointed out in his distinctive slow southern drawl.

Thom leaned far to one side to get his hand into his pocket. He emerged with the small square box. The kind of jewelers box that usually contained one thing—a ring.

"Holy shit," Brody hissed as he obviously figured out Thom's intentions just from the telltale size and shape of the small black velvet box in his hand.

His friend's reaction had Thom's pulse pounding as his thoughts reeled. "I know. I'm crazy, right? I shouldn't do this. I can't do this."

Since theirs had become quite a conversation it was a good thing they were seated in the way back, and that they'd all been there too long to care much about what the speaker up front was saying or if they missed hearing some of it.

"Whoa, there." Brody held up both hands palm forward. "Now wait a minute, bro. Step on back. I didn't say that."

"No, you're right." Thom shoved the ring box back into one of the gusseted leg pockets in his pants, as if putting it away could or would save him from himself and his bad decisions when it came to women.

Shit. How could one comment from Brody have Thom ready to completely change the direction of his own future? Not just his future, but Ginny's too.

The answer was, it hadn't been Brody. Thom had been having some pretty serious second thoughts about this decision in the first place.

No, that wasn't exactly accurate. He had no doubts that he loved Ginny. What he couldn't stomp down were his fears. Mainly, the fear the relationship would implode, just like his first marriage had.

Was it better to leave things as they were rather than try to move forward and mess it up?

No. He wanted her. Wanted to be with her. So why was he feeling more trepidation at the idea of proposing to Ginny than he felt during a firefight?

He truly loved Ginny. He had since that fateful winter he'd literally crashed into her life during a Christmas Eve snowstorm.

It physically hurt him to be away from her. He counted the days, and then the hours, until they could see each other again.

It made no sense for him to be nearly paralyzed with fear now that he had the engagement ring in his possession. Ginny was nothing like his ex-wife. Just as his relationship with Ginny was nothing like that with his ex had been.

There was no doubt in his mind that he wanted to be with Ginny until the day he died. But unlike his military career, in which he'd steadily attained the advancements he'd worked for, marriage was the one area in his life where he'd tried and failed—and failed in a spectacularly miserable way. Or was it a miserably spectacular way?

However he thought of it, it had been bad. Epically bad.

Even so, it wasn't as if SEALs didn't get married. Plenty operators he knew did. A few even stayed married. But Thom and Debbie's divorce had been particularly nasty.

His ex-wife had left him so penniless the only real surprise here was that he'd saved enough money to buy an engagement ring for Ginny.

It wasn't just himself and his own feelings factoring into the decision. There were his kids to consider and his ex-wife's overbearing control over his visitation with them.

Then there was his schedule, which sent him all over the world at the whim of the military.

And there was Ginny and the hurdles on her end of this long distance relationship. She had a life in Connecticut, far away from Virginia. Her family was up north and from what he'd learned over the years they'd been dating, her mother was not going to be at all happy at the thought of her only child moving away to be with him.

He was away a lot. To ask Ginny to wait for him, alone in base housing, wondering where he was and when he'd be back, didn't seem fair to her. Or to her family who was used to having her close by.

In light of all that, why he was nervous was no longer the question. What had made him even think he could make this work? *That* was the question.

He glanced toward the front of the theater. This thing had to be over soon.

Checking the time on his cell, he discovered that it wasn't as late as he'd assumed. It only felt as if they'd been there forever.

Sighing, Thom slumped in his seat.

Leaning closer, Brody said, "Hey, listen to me. When we get the hell out of here you and I are gonna go somewhere and talk this through. A'ight?"

Thom nodded, giving in. "Okay. Thanks."

He didn't know how talking to Brody could help, but it certainly couldn't hurt.

It wasn't as if he had a better idea. Or something better to do. Not with Ginny four hundred miles away. Four hundred and four to be exact. He'd counted each and every mile the too few times he'd driven to be with her.

Before he talked himself out of this proposal, abandoned his plan and had to ask the jeweler about his return policy, Thom figured he should at least be open to reasoning things out, rationally, possibly over a drink since he sure felt as if he could use one.

Hell after his flipping out on his teammate, on top of the boredom of the past few hours, Thom was pretty sure Brody could use a beer too . . . or something stronger.

Given how crazed Thom felt at the moment, bourbon straight up definitely wasn't out of the question.

The cell, still in his hand so he could obsess about the time, vibrated.

There was a rustling of motion and the glow of blue light around him as other men checked their own phones. Next to him, Brody reached for his pocket too.

Thom didn't need to look at the display to know what was happening. All the signs were there. A platoon's worth of SEALs getting simultaneous texts in the middle of an all-hands briefing could mean only one thing. They were getting called in for something.

So much for his planned visit with Ginny.

"Shit." Thom breathed out the curse, low and mostly to himself.

"Yup." Brody's agreement as he bent over the

cell in his hand told Thom his teammate had heard him and agreed with the sentiment. The cell's display illuminated Brody's face in the dim theater before he clicked it off. "Time to go."

Brody stood. Thom and about a dozen other guys did the same.

This was clearly one of those good news, bad news kinds of situations. The good news was they got to leave this eternally long required briefing. The bad news was there was no telling what they were being recalled for or what they were about to walk into.

This—getting yanked away on next to no notice to travel God only knew where for an assignment of indeterminate danger for an undisclosed amount of time *if* he came home at all—was exactly why Thom shouldn't even think about proposing to Ginny.

It was also exactly why he wanted to. Why he *had* to.

If this morning were to be the last day he woke on this earth, he would have wanted to wake next to her.

As he walked shoulder to shoulder with Brody toward the meeting room, he felt calmer about his decision to propose than he had all day.

That considering his own death had settled his restless mind was pretty screwed up. But then again, the men who opted for a career in Naval Special Warfare didn't tend to think the same as others.

Of course, his calm could also stem from knowing that thanks to getting recalled he had a temporary reprieve from having to do anything regarding the ring in his pocket.

Now that he wasn't a nervous wreck and his obsessing was done—for the time being—he turned his mind to possible reasons for the summons from command.

"What do you think this is about?" Thom asked Brody, even though they'd all know soon enough anyway.

Brody blew out a loud, lip-flapping breath. "The way things have been lately, there ain't no telling."

Thom sniffed in agreement. "That's the truth."

They'd all been on high alert and told to expect the possibility of more high profile terrorist attacks in larger cities since Ramadan was about to begin.

Besides that, any number of things could have happened anywhere in the world while they'd been in the briefing. Or nothing had happened but some politician had decided that now was the time to call on them for a showy mission to grab some press.

In spite of the need for secrecy, the media loved to report on SEAL Team 6, and the politicians taking credit for the team's successes didn't hate the public exposure.

It didn't take long to cover the distance from the theater to the meeting room. When Thom walked through the door he could see his commander, Grant Milton, was already in the front of the room flipping through some papers in a file folder.

Grant glanced up as operators filed into the room. He looked like he was in a hurry to get started, which gave Thom a clue as to the urgency of the situation. Luckily, everyone called in should have been on base for the all-hands meeting so they wouldn't have to wait long for anyone.

The room filled quickly, if not quietly, and soon Grant had signaled for attention. Silence—save for the scrape of a chair or the shuffle of a boot against the floor—fell upon the group.

Grant began, "At zero-three-hundred hours, Kabul time, insurgents attacked a compound run by a Swedish aid group. They beheaded the Afghan guard and proceeded to the second floor where they shot and killed one German female. A second female, an American citizen residing with her husband in Finland, was at the compound and has been reported missing."

As Thom sat and listened to Grant, the reason for the recall and the urgency became apparent. There was nothing they could do for the two victims who'd been killed, but they could hope to find the American woman who'd been taken.

The stress was clear on Grant's face as he spoke and Thom could guess why. It was only recently that the team had gone in to rescue a female US aid worker being held for ransom in Somalia.

That had been a tough one. After months of captivity, the American woman had been underweight, dehydrated and in imminent danger from a raging fever and infection left untreated. Not to mention the emotional damage done to her in addition to the physical.

Thom suspected that it was memories of that mission that had Grant wearing such a grave expression now. Because though the commander was a private man and had kept it surprisingly quiet, the team knew Grant was now in a romantic relationship with the woman they'd rescued.

How would Thom feel if Ginny was ever taken or in danger? He could only imagine. Actually, he didn't want to even do that. He'd lose his mind.

"At this time, no group has claimed responsibility, however, we have our suspicions."

Next to Thom, Brody said under his breath, "Me too."

"Mm, hm," Thom agreed.

The Afghan Taliban wasn't typically known for beheadings but ISIS, aka *Daesh,* sure was. This event had all the markers of the Islamic State.

"Officials in country are working on some leads. They should have more by the time we land. We go wheels up in an hour."

The general noise in the room increased exponentially after Grant dismissed them to get ready for departure.

"Looks like our talk about *that*," Brody glanced down at Thom's pocket where the ring still resided, "is gonna have to wait."

Thom's thoughts exactly as they walked toward the cages to grab their shit. Given he wouldn't be proposing because he was about to fly off to Afghanistan to chase after a group of jihadists who'd gladly kill or die for their cause he wasn't sure if he felt grateful or terrified over the delay.

CHAPTER THREE

Ginny balled her hand into a fist to keep from screaming or tearing out her own hair.

Yoga breathing, Ginny. Deep breath in. Slow and steady, big breath out.

She calmed herself enough to not blow up at her mother's comment as she said, "Mom, it's just easier for me to go down to visit Thom than it is for him to come up here."

Her mother's sniff of disagreement or disapproval—probably both—was audible through the phone.

"So you're just going to miss every holiday with your family and spend it down *there* with *him*?"

She took another deep breath to temper her rising annoyance. "I was with you for Christmas and for Mother's Day."

Ginny considered those the two biggest holidays each year for a daughter to be with her mother. But if her mother had her way, they'd be celebrating every holiday on the calendar, right down to Groundhog's Day.

This latest rant had been brought on by her mother's hissy fit about Ginny's plans to be with Thom in Virginia for the long Memorial Day weekend at the end of this month.

"It's fine. You do whatever you'd like." Now there was hurt as well as anger in her mother's tone.

Ginny let out a sigh trying to remember this attitude stemmed from her mother's love and desire to see her. If she didn't keep that in mind, she'd lose her temper for sure. There'd be no coming back from what would no doubt be one hell of a ugly fight.

"There's a chance I might not even be going," she assured her mom.

Given what Thom did for a living, that was the complete truth. He could—and had—gotten called away on next to no notice.

She'd learned long ago to not book a flight in advance. Paying one airline change fee had taught her that lesson early on in their relationship. Dealing with Thom's guilt and apologies because he had been the cause of the cancellation of her visit was worse than the exorbitant airline fee.

Now she usually hopped on the Amtrak and enjoyed the scenic ride from Connecticut to Virginia. And honestly, she really did enjoy it. With the peace and quiet and nothing but time and her laptop on those long train rides she'd even gotten quite a bit of work done.

The literary romance of the rails, like in the

grand old days of travel a hundred years ago, inspired her. It was as if she'd stepped back to the time of F. Scott Fitzgerald and Hemingway, but without all the boozing. Or as if she was Harry Potter, embarking on a great adventure from Platform 9 ¾.

But neither her mother nor her best friend Molly understood all that. They both thought Thom should come to her. Or pay for her to fly to him. Apparently, his being off saving the world didn't help her friend's and family's opinion of him.

At Ginny's comment that the trip might be canceled anyway, her mother let out a *humph* that spoke volumes. All was definitely not forgiven.

Thom might have the daunting duty of combatting bad guys all over the globe, but Ginny had a battle of her own closer to home to deal with. Unlike terrorists, who favored bombs and bullets, her mother's weapon of choice was guilt.

Luckily Ginny had been fighting this war her entire adult life. She was getting pretty good at it. Tired of it, but proficient in diffusing the situation nonetheless.

"How about I come over this weekend and cook you and Dad dinner?" she offered.

"We're busy Saturday night."

"All right, what about Sunday? I could come over early and spend the day."

"I guess that would be okay." In spite of herself, her mother was softening. Ginny heard it in her tone.

"It's settled then. I'll see you Sunday. And I'll touch base with you before then to plan the menu."

"Okay. I'll go tell your father." Much brighter now, her mother sounded genuinely happy.

"Good. You do that and I'll talk to you soon. Bye."

The moment her mother said goodbye Ginny punched the cell's screen to disconnect the call. She dropped the phone to the sofa.

She'd traded all day Sunday for a moment's peace today. She only hoped the truce lasted for a while because she still had every intention of spending the long weekend with Thom in Virginia.

An alert had her glancing down at the cell on the cushion next to her. One glimpse of the display had her sighing as she read the text from Thom.

Don't buy your train ticket yet.

Crap. Maybe she wouldn't be away for Memorial Day after all.

Drawing in a deep breath she grabbed for the phone and dialed his number. He never could tell her much, but she hoped she'd be able to get some information from him.

More than that, if he'd been called in, who knew when she'd be able to talk to him again?

The phone rang once before he picked up. "Hey, baby. I'm so sorry."

The level of background noise told her he was busy doing something and surrounded by others probably doing the same thing. Experience had her guessing he was getting ready to leave.

Over the couple of years they'd been dating she'd learned to read the signs. The low drone of other male voices nearby. The rustle and clink of equipment being loaded into packs. The clanging of the metal doors where they kept their stuff locked up. Thom breathing heavier than usual as he rushed to do what he needed to while speaking to her.

Yup. She could kiss this visit goodbye.

They'd be going on three months since she'd seen him. Saddened by that realization, she still tried to sound upbeat as she said, "It's okay."

"No, it's not. I was looking forward to seeing you."

That made her smile through the mist forming in her eyes. "Me too. We'll make new plans."

"Well, I'm not writing this trip off as dead in the water quite yet. I'm gonna do everything I can to be able to see you soon. I just . . . don't know right now."

"I know. I'll be here waiting whenever you find out." It wasn't like she had anything else to do.

"I know you will be."

Thank God as a freelance editor she could work from anywhere and could set her own schedule. If she had a job with regular office hours and scheduled vacation days, they'd really be screwed.

"Hey. Have I told you how much I love you?" he asked for probably the hundredth time since they'd been dating.

"Nope. Never." She smiled because no matter how corny their little private joke was, and no matter how many times he'd told her how much he loved her, she'd gladly hear it a thousand times more.

"Well, I do. Look, I'm gonna have to go."

"I love you. So much." She rushed to say it as the panic set in.

After he said goodbye she wouldn't know when he'd be back or when she'd hear from him again. She wouldn't let her mind go to that place where she thought about how he might not return. If she let herself obsess about that reality every time he left she'd drive herself crazy.

"And I love you. So much. I don't know when it will be but I'll call you as soon as I can," he said.

"Okay."

"Bye, baby."

Swallowing hard she said, "Bye."

The silence on the line after he'd hung up had her eyes stinging from the tears trying to spill out.

Being in love wasn't supposed to hurt so much. Was it?

Ginny gave herself a mental slap. She was stronger than this. They'd been making this long distance relationship work for years. It was worth it. Thom was worth it.

It would all work out. She'd see him soon enough and it would be even more special when she did because of the time they'd been apart.

But damn she missed him so much it physically hurt. She rubbed a hand over the place in her chest where her heart ached.

Then a thought hit her that made it all feel even worse. She wasn't going to Virginia to see Thom *but* she'd still have to spend all day Sunday at her parents' house.

Crap.

CHAPTER FOUR

After landing at Bagram Airfield at zero-dark-thirty the platoon had gone directly into an emergency briefing on base, followed by the drive to where they were now, at the German Embassy in Kabul.

Good thing Thom had drugged himself with a sleeping pill for the flight so he arrived rested, because even though it could seem at times that command moved at a sloth's pace on missions, this time it appeared as if they were ready to rock and roll.

Time was of the essence if they were going to find this woman alive.

While the dozen SEALs had been in transit, representatives from the usual three-letter US governmental organizations, along with the local Afghan officials and the German authorities, had been busy combining efforts and information.

Between drone and satellite surveillance, chatter on the wires and rumors among the locals, they'd been able to determine a probable location for the group holding the American woman. The same group who had killed the German worker and beheaded the local Afghan guard, which was probably the reason there was far more sharing of resources between the three countries' authorities than usual.

Of course, without hard intel nothing was a definite. More, what was an accurate location today could be useless tomorrow if the group chose to move to another hideout.

It was a delicate dance between taking the time to prepare properly for the highest chance of success, while also moving fast enough to get to her before she was moved or worse, killed.

Staring down at the plans laid out on the conference table, drawings that showed the layout of the compound where they suspected the terrorists to be, Thom shook his head. "I don't like how no one's demanded a ransom. It could mean she's already dead."

Next to him, Brody shot Thom a sideways glance. "I don't like how we haven't discussed what we'd planned to discuss before we got recalled. You okay? You got your head in the game?"

"Of course, I do." Thom frowned at Brody.

Brody lifted a brow. "You sure?"

Thom glanced around. They were on a break so the room that had been packed with SEALs for the past hour was nearly empty now as most of the platoon had gone to hit the head or grab sustenance.

Even so, Thom kept his voice low as he said, "Yeah, I'm sure."

He'd managed to concentrate on the mission and keep his mind off the ring he'd left locked away with his stuff back on base in Virginia until Brody had brought it up again.

He leveled a glare at his skeptical friend. "I know the plan backward and forward. I could probably draw the layout of the location to scale from memory if I had to."

Brody nodded. "Just checking."

Scowling, Thom was sorry he'd ever showed Brody that ring. "Well, no need. Just because I bought the damn thing doesn't mean I have to decide right away. Hell, I can wait another year if I want."

Dipping his head, Brody said, "Yup. You sure can."

"Or I can go home and ask her right away." Thom lifted his shoulders in a shrug.

"Mm, hm. You could." Brody tipped his head again.

For some reason Brody's easy agreement with everything Thom said was pissing him off. Thom huffed out a breath. "The point is I don't have to think about it at all and definitely not right now while prepping for a raid."

"Yup, I can see you're not thinking about it. Not one bit." Brody's lips twitched.

In questioning him about being distracted, all Brody had done was raise the issue and cause Thom to become distracted.

He drew his brows low, hating that his supposed

friend had planted a seed of doubt in his brain. "Fuck you, Brody."

At that, Brody broke into a wide smile. "Love you too, bro. Hey, where'd they say that cafeteria was?" Brody asked, changing subjects like they weren't in the middle of a serious discussion.

Thom had just been about to further lay into Brody for bringing up the subject of the engagement in the first place, but he had to admit, he could eat.

If command decided it was time to move out, decent food might not come again for many hours. "First floor. But I saw a food place across the street when we came in. Maybe we can check that out too."

"Sounds good to me." Brody took a single step to come around to Thom's side of the table, which was closer to the door, when a blast rocked the embassy.

Knocked off balance, Thom braced his palms on the table.

The building shook but this was no earthquake. He'd been close to enough explosions during his career that he recognized the sound and the feel of one.

Brody's eyes widened as he too grabbed for the table. "What the fuck?"

Thom strode toward the door, Brody in his wake.

Across the hall, more of the platoon stacked up on either side of the windows facing the front of the building. From that vantage point—pressed up against the wall—they'd be able to see out into the street while having some cover.

"What was it?" Thom asked the group in general.

"Looks like a vehicle-born IED," Rocky Mangiano answered without turning.

"A big one. A tanker truck, judging by the wreckage. What's left of it." Craig Dawson, formerly *the new guy* and more recently *the kid*, shook his head and glanced at Thom over his shoulder. "It's bad."

Inching closer, Brody glanced out the window. "Damn."

To plan an attack in the city's most highly protected area was a ballsy move on the part of the bomber and he'd succeeded, proving that, obviously, the Afghan Security Forces *security* wasn't secure enough.

Another blast sounded, not as loud. It was smaller or far enough away that it didn't shake the building, but it was a blast nonetheless.

"Shit. Another one." Thom edged toward the window to see for himself.

"It's on the other side of the city." Dawson tipped his chin toward a plume of smoke, barely visible, rising into the air.

The US embassy was only about half a mile away from where they stood in the German embassy, but in the opposite direction from the last explosion.

They should stay completely clear of the windows, but Thom dared to lean in and got a good look at the carnage below.

There were a lot of casualties. Some not moving. Others, bloodied and obviously hurt, attempted to walk or crawl to get away from the area.

They'd been warned to expect attacks on

Western cities during the Muslim holy month. But this was Kabul. Muslims attacking Muslims during their holiest time of the year was the kind of insanity that pointed to the Islamic State. Although the Taliban was always a possibility.

There were ninety-eight recognized terrorist organizations worldwide. Twenty of them known to be in Afghanistan. Until someone took responsibility, it was all an educated guess and at this point it didn't really matter.

Who was responsible was something to be considered after they'd dealt with trying to save as many lives as possible.

It was hard to get a clear view of the area but Thom visually searched for more threats. It wouldn't be out of the ordinary for the bomb to be only part one of the attack.

Two blasts indicated this was a coordinated effort, not the actions of a lone wolf. There could be more terrorists out there, armed and ready to attack. Snipers lying in wait to pick off the first responders one by one.

Normally, he'd pay close attention to the rooftops and upper level windows of any surrounding buildings but the explosives had done a hell of a lot of damage to all the structures nearby. And it was nearly impossible to see the buildings still standing farther away through the smoke and dust in the air.

The entire area was in ruins with vehicles mangled and buildings crumbling. Just down the block, at what must have been ground zero for the explosion, was a crater at least a dozen feet deep.

Then there was the human toll. This was the Afghan capital's diplomatic district on a weekday during rush hour. Banks, embassies, government buildings, markets—and all the people who'd be among them.

They needed to get down there and do what they could to help until emergency vehicles arrived. Even from this distance he could see the casualties were horrendous.

His unit might be trained to kill but they were also well trained in first aid in the field. In situations like this, a simple tourniquet could mean the difference between life and death for the victims.

He'd just had the thought when Grant topped the staircase. "Get downstairs and outside. Triage the wounded. Help whoever can be saved."

"And if we encounter a threat?" James *Mack* McIntyre asked.

It was a good question. Thom had been wondering about the rules of engagement himself. They hadn't been briefed for how to respond to an attack while inside a foreign embassy located in one of the busiest and supposedly safest neighborhoods in the capital.

Grant's nostrils flared as he said, "Do what's necessary."

As the sound of booted feet thundered down the stairs Thom couldn't help but think that had the explosion come a couple of hours earlier, as they were arriving, it could be him and his platoon lying in the street bleeding out. And if it had come one minute later as he and Brody crossed the street to get food, it could have been him down there in bloody pieces.

It was a sobering thought, one that had his heart pounding until he pushed through the door and out into the sunlight clouded by dust and smoke.

All the *what ifs* that had been running through his brain fled. He had the reality of the bomb's aftermath to deal with.

After crossing the courtyard and running through the gate of the high walls, which had done much to protect the embassy from the blast, he saw the full extent of the horror close up.

As the sound of police sirens in the distance grew louder, his boots crunched on shards of glass. He skirted the worst of the debris in the rubble-clogged street.

At the sight of the first bloodied victim, training and adrenaline took over and he went to work to save who he could. Hopefully, there was no one out there lying in wait, set on preventing him from doing that.

CHAPTER FIVE

The waiting and wondering was driving Ginny crazy.

She'd been walking around with the cell phone in her hand for the past two weeks. All day, every day. Bringing it with her to the bathroom. Propping it up within reach of the shower stall. Obsessively charging it and checking it had signal. Sleeping with it next to her head with the volume on high so she wouldn't miss a call should it come while she slept.

What else could she do? If she missed a call from Thom while he was away she'd just die.

She remained attached to the device like it was another appendage even though Molly did roll her eyes at Ginny's neurotic dependence on the device every time they were together.

Easy for Molly to judge. She didn't have a boyfriend running off to God only knew where doing life threatening things Ginny wasn't even allowed to know about.

Molly didn't have to maintain a long distance relationship where the only connection was contingent upon a stupid electronic device—or a smart device, as the case may be.

In fact, Molly was currently between serious boyfriends and having a great time going out on dates with practically a different guy each weekend, so she didn't have to worry about anything at all.

A realization slapped Ginny in the face like a bucket of cold water. It was only a couple of years ago, before she'd met Thom, that she'd been the one going out on dates with a different guy each week from one dating website or another, and absolutely hating it. And she had been insanely envious of Molly who'd been the one with the steady boyfriend.

Now, the situation was reversed but Ginny still envied aspects of her friend's carefree, worry-free life. Apparently it was true that the grass was always greener on the other side of the fence.

Ginny was so busy ranting inside her own head about so many things that when her cell phone rang while in her hand she jumped.

Her gaze shot to the display as Thom's name and photo appeared and she nearly dropped the phone trying to swipe the screen to answer the call.

She was breathless as she pressed it to her ear and said, "Hi."

"Hey, baby." He sounded less excited to be speaking with her than she was to finally hear from him. Ginny wrote that off to his being tired.

No matter how he sounded, it was an enormous relief to hear his voice. To know he was safe.

"Are you home?" she asked. Sometimes he called while in transit when he could find cell signal or internet while traveling.

"Yeah. We got in real late last night."

"Oh." Ginny glanced at the clock. It was already the afternoon. He'd been home for almost a day and he was just getting around to calling her now? She pressed her lips together, determined to not comment on that and decided to change the subject. "So have you thought about a date for our visit?"

Memorial Day weekend had come and gone, and he'd been away for it, but having new plans would make her feel so much better about having missed their visit.

"Um . . ." That single syllable from Thom's lips had Ginny's hopes falling. "Hold off on that for a little bit."

She bit her lip before saying, "Okay."

At a loss for what else to say, she remained silent. She knew better than to ask about where he'd been or what he'd done. It was pointless to press him to make firm plans for a visit. Experience had taught her that when dealing with the military, plans changed—often.

She heard the noise of male voices around him and asked, "Do you have to go?"

"Yeah, I should. I'll call you back later, okay?"

Ginny drew in a breath through her nose and let it out. "Okay."

"I love you." Those words from his mouth usually never failed to soften her heart, even through the worst of the disappointment and sadness. But today, they didn't do as much as usual to make her feel better.

Even so, she said, "I love you too."

"Bye, baby."

"Bye." She'd just said the word when the cell went silent as he disconnected.

Now that the relief from learning he was safe was starting to fade, she went cold inside.

Ginny tossed the cell to the sofa cushion and stood. She stalked toward the kitchen area, freed from carrying the cell in her hand for the first time in weeks.

She'd see him again, one day, and the moment she did she'd forget what this overwhelming disappointment felt like, but right now, it was time for some comfort food.

CHAPTER SIX

Thom disconnected the call with Ginny and walked to the break room.

He threw his six-foot frame into the chair and sank back into the cushions of the chair next to Brody.

Brody took one look at Thom's face and said, "Call not go well?"

"Nope." Thom had heard the tone of Ginny's voice change from the start of the call to the end.

She was losing patience with him, with this whole long distance thing, and he didn't blame her. Relationships were hard enough when two people lived in the same state. Forget about with hundreds of miles in between them.

"Need to talk?" Brody asked.

"Nope."

"A'ighty, then." The energy drink was barely up to Brody's mouth when Thom spun in the chair to face him.

"If I don't ask her soon, she's going to give up on us. I can feel it."

Brody lowered the can again. "Is that the reason you wanna get married? So she won't break up with you?"

"No, of course not. That's not it. I want to be with her. Married to her. More than anything."

"Good God almighty, you're making my head hurt. Bro, if you want to marry her, then ask her."

Thom threw his hands in the air. "I can't get to her. I'm trapped here for who knows how long thanks to this new assignment. And I'm sure as hell not asking her to come down knowing we'll likely be gone again soon."

It just figured that sometimes they'd go months between ops with nothing to do but train at Little Creek to keep their skills sharp, but now that he really needed to see Ginny, the platoon was getting back-to-back assignments.

"Hey, I just said to do it. I didn't say it would be easy. You'll figure it out."

That advice was less than useless.

"Great. Thanks." Scowling, Thom pressed back against the cushions, frustrated with the situation and annoyed with Brody whether he deserved it or not.

"Sure. Anytime," Brody said, his tone upbeat.

Thom had to hand it to him, the man didn't get insulted easily, even with as hard as Thom tried.

But Brody was right about one thing, Thom was going to have to figure out how to make this work and soon.

First chance he got, he'd ask Grant for leave. If and when he got it approved, he was jumping in the SUV and heading the seven hours north to lock this relationship with Ginny down. Make her at least his fiancé if not his wife.

Dawson stuck his head into the break room. "Yeo. Meeting room. They're ready to start."

It seemed their short reprieve between briefings was done.

"A'ight. Thanks." Brody hoisted himself out of the chair and pitched his can into the recycling bin. "Break's over. Time to go."

This morning had been a post-mission debrief about Kabul. They had reviewed everything that had gone wrong and went over how they could handle it better next time. This briefing they were walking into now was to prepare them for the next mission.

Usually the action was scarce enough to make the guys itch to get going somewhere. Thom hoped this new heightened level of activity was seasonal— just a result of Ramadan—and not the new normal. Because the way things had been going lately, a couple of months of good old boring trainings were looking pretty damn good.

Thom hoisted his tired body out of the chair and followed Brody out the door and into the meeting room.

By the time he arrived, he saw the man reputed to be the platoon's computer guru, Will Weber, up in front of the room. With him stood Grant and the other unit's commanding officer Mike Groenning.

There were empty seats on either side of Rocky,

so Thom pulled out one chair while Brody took the other.

"What's Willy Wonka doing up there in front?" Brody asked, tipping his chin toward Will.

Poor Will had turned blue during drown proofing in BUD/S making him look just like the girl who'd ate too much candy in the Willy Wonka movie. After that, with the first name William he had no hope of avoiding the nickname.

Rocky lifted his shoulders. "No clue. You know as much as I do."

Thom leaned forward to answer Brody next to Rocky. "Might be computer related somehow if they brought in the computer wizard and his toys."

Currently Will had not one but two oversized laptops set on the table in front of him and was punching keys with one hand on each keyboard. Behind him, the blank screen was bright white with the illumination of the projector.

"I'd say you're right." Rocky laughed. "Damn, look at all that shit he's got."

Brody shook his head. "Yeah, well, he can keep it. I don't even like using a damn smart phone. I miss my old flip phone."

"You're nuts." Rocky snorted, shaking his head at Brody.

"Everybody here?" Grant asked in a voice loud and commanding enough to silence the low chatter in the room.

Next to him, Groenning nodded. "Looks like. Go ahead, Weber."

"All right, guys. So here he is. Meet your next worst nightmare." A picture flashed on the screen of a child and the room broke out in laughter.

Fitz, a guy from Will's unit, said, "A kid?"

"He was a kid *then*." Will glanced from the group to the screen. "On screen, my friends, is the last known photo of Osama Bin Laden's son, Hamza. The only son born to him by his third and reputedly favorite wife. He's about twenty-eight years old now and the next best hope for al-Qaeda."

"Then why are there no current photos?" The question came from another of Will's teammates, Tompkins.

"Because he's smart, making him a triple threat." Will spun away from the screen to face them. "Hamza can trace his bloodline back directly to Mohammad on his mother's side. He's Osama's son. And, as I said, he's no dummy." Will counted off the three points on his fingers. "More, unlike others in the terrorist group, he's never been critical of Daesh so he hadn't made an enemy of that group's supporters. And he's encouraging more violent, less coordinated, lone wolf violence against the West in a clear attempt to woo away the followers from the weakened Islamic State."

Grant took a step forward. "He's got the heart and the ear of the *mujahedeen*. That, combined with his lineage, makes Hamza the one figure who could unify the fractured Islamist militants and that makes him dangerous."

"And he's still pissed about Abbottabad and vowing revenge for the death of his father and half brother," Will added. "He's not ever seen but he sure as hell is heard and what he's saying is resonating with the younger generation of jihadists.

In fact, Hamza posted a statement calling for attacks against major Western cities just two weeks before the bombing in Manchester."

"Damn," Rocky blew out the curse softly beneath his breath.

"In addition to there being no confirmed recent photos, his location is also unknown," Groenning added.

"However . . ." Will stepped toward his computers again. "I have a lead."

Thom smiled. He had no doubt. If anyone could find Osama's heir apparent, Will could.

The picture on screen changed to a satellite image of a stately building with a walled courtyard. "This is where I believe Hamza lived for part of the time his father had him stashed away in Iran for safe keeping after 9/11. Right up until just before we took out Osama and Khalid in Abbottabad. It belongs to a family friend. It's also where I think we'll find clues to where Hamza could be now."

"Mark your calendars, boys." Grant grinned. "We're going in during the next new moon."

Sad but true, Thom knew exactly when the next new moon would be. These new moon raids had begun to become the norm.

Just this calendar year there had already been two. Both in Yemen. The first, in January, had become a clusterfuck of epic proportions and had ended with a flag draped coffin for one of his SEAL brothers and not much, if any, useful intelligence. The second, in Marib in May, had been successful, yielding a slew of information.

Given those odds of success, fifty-fifty by his

calculations, Thom knew what he was going to have to do.

Grant was moments away from dismissing them, he hoped. The two commanders were up there in deep discussion with each other while the dozen men in the room cooled their heels and waited to be cut loose.

Thom sat on the edge of his seat waiting for that moment and when it finally came, he almost sprinted to get to Grant, bobbing and weaving against the tide of guys trying to get out of the room while he was trying to get farther in.

"Sir, can I talk to you?"

"Sure." Grant nodded. "What's up?"

"I'd like to officially request leave to travel to see Ginny in Connecticut."

Grant pressed his lips together and drew in a deep breath. "We're heading out to Iran. There's no doubt about it. Unless someone way above my pay grade calls it off, this op is a go."

"Yes, sir. That's why I thought now might be a good time to take a couple of days. We won't be at the top of the list to get sent anywhere else because we're scheduled to leave so soon for Iran."

Shaking his head, Grant laughed. "That's actually some real good reasoning you came up with there."

Not sure if it was a compliment or not, Thom said, "Uh, thank you."

"Just a couple of days?" Grant asked.

"Yes." If he had to he'd drive up one day, ask her, and drive home the next. Not ideal but better than nothing.

"Mind if I ask what's so pressing you have to get to Connecticut? And keep in mind you can tell me to mind my own damn business, though that might not help sway me in favor of giving you this leave." Grant grinned.

"I'm going there to propose to her."

Grant's eyes widened. "Wow. Not what I was expecting."

"I'm not surprised." Thom let out a short laugh. He knew his divorce and the aftermath was no secret. "I know it's last minute but I don't wanna wait if I don't have to. She had plans to come down here to see me over Memorial Day—"

"And we were in Afghanistan instead." Grant nodded.

"Yeah. I figure I owe her a visit and I'd like to do it before we leave."

"Your parents are up there too, correct?" Grant asked.

"Yes, sir. In Massachusetts. About two hours away from where Ginny lives."

Lips pressed together, Grant nodded. "Command allows you ninety-six hours to visit parents before deploying. I'll extend that and give you the whole weekend instead of making you be back by Saturday. Be back on base and at the team meeting at zero-eight-hundred Monday.

Thom's eyes widened. "Thank you, sir. I don't know what to say."

"No need to say anything. Now get out of here and have fun."

"Thank you, sir. I will."

He turned for the door and heard Grant say,

"Keep your cell on. Just in case."

Glancing over his shoulder, Thom said, "Always do, sir. Just in case."

Monday. He had the whole weekend.

Even though he was exhausted from running on next to no sleep, he practically sprinted to his vehicle in the parking lot.

First thing, he'd head to the house and spend an hour or so with the kids. He hadn't seen them yet since getting back from Kabul and had already called to ask if he could stop by tonight. If he canceled, Debbie would no doubt punish him next time he asked by not letting him see them on a day that he wasn't scheduled to.

After that he'd head home, throw some clothes in a bag, grab a few hours sleep and get on the road by dawn to avoid the morning rush hour traffic around DC.

He'd be in Stamford with Ginny well before lunch tomorrow. Perfect.

She was going to be shocked to see him standing at her door. When he whipped out that ring, even more so. Just the thought had him smiling.

CHAPTER SEVEN

Ginny slid her reading glasses higher up her nose and tried desperately to concentrate on the manuscript she was being paid to proofread.

She'd started taking on proofing jobs, in addition to her usual editing, because the rent on her crappy one room apartment above a storefront stretched her budget to nearly the breaking point each month. If she wanted to have any money for travel to see Thom, she needed to bring in some extra cash.

Usually printing out the manuscript and reading the paper copy made it easier to see the mistakes than trying to do it on a computer screen. Today, not so much.

Knowing her mind had wandered, she sighed and forced herself to read the prior paragraph one more time.

Sure enough, there was a mistake. Marking it with her red pen, she started to wonder if she'd missed anything else.

She should probably start the chapter over to be sure. Hell, with her mind all over the place today, she really should go back to page one.

A more diligent person might do that, even if it would take her an extra hour, at least, to finish the job. She'd have to decide if she was that kind of person later, after she'd gotten through some more of this damn book that seemed as if it would never end.

Still in the pajama bottoms she'd slept in and a fresh T-shirt she'd thrown on after getting up—her usual work at home outfit—she snuggled deeper into the sofa cushion. Her bare toes were feeling chilly on this cool, rainy June day, so she pulled the throw over her legs and settled in to get down to work.

Resolved and settled, she might have been able to concentrate, if there hadn't been a knock on the door.

"Shit." She was going to have to answer that.

Sliding off her glasses, she glanced down at herself and decided she looked good enough. At least she had on a bra and had gotten around to brushing her teeth and washing her face this morning.

It could be Molly or it could be a package delivery. Either way, whoever had arrived unannounced before noon would have to take her as they found her.

She peered through the apartment door's peephole to see who the unlucky person would be.

When she saw him, she sucked in a breath.

Yanking on the doorknob, she remembered the lock and wrestled to get it open, before flinging the door wide.

She was in Thom's arms in seconds, airborne, her legs wrapped around his waist as he held her close and tight.

"I missed you." His voice was muffled as he spoke against her hair.

"I missed you." She pulled back far enough to locate his lips and planted a quick hard kiss on him before saying, "Why didn't you tell me you were coming?"

"I wanted to surprise you."

"But when I talked to you yesterday you didn't—"

"I asked for leave," he said as he took another step into the room while still holding her. "I had to see you. I couldn't wait."

She'd seen that look in his eyes before and knew what it meant. They were on the way to the bed. She glanced back toward the door, still open to the hallway. "Wait. The door."

He pivoted to shoulder the door shut then turned back toward her bedroom—or rather toward the folding screen that separated the bed area from the living area.

She was about to remind him to lock the deadbolt—habit from being a woman living alone—when she remembered who she was with and stopped worrying. If anyone dared to come into her apartment uninvited while Thom was there, she had a feeling they'd be very sorry they did.

Besides, there were much better things to think

about than hypothetical burglars, such as how good his muscles felt as she pressed close . . . and how good they'd look once she got him out of the T-shirt and jeans.

Thom didn't set her feet back on the ground until they were next to the bed. With his hands free from holding her he tangled them in her hair and leaned low. "Need you so bad."

The feeling was mutual. She chose to show him rather than telling him and stood on tiptoe to close the short distance to his lips.

This—these moments—were what made it all okay. The separation. The distance. The frequent lack of communication. It all faded away the moment they finally saw each other after being apart.

But it was also at that very moment that the clock started ticking down to the inevitable time when they'd have to part again.

How long did they have this time? How long before she'd be saying goodbye to him again for weeks, if not months? Twenty-four hours? Forty-eight hours?

It was never long when he came to see her, which was why she preferred going to him. Besides, she hated knowing seven hours of his short precious leave had been wasted on the road as he drove to be with her.

Thinking of saying goodbye when they'd just said hello flooded her eyes with tears. As he kissed her and roamed her body with his hands she desperately tried to keep the tears from spilling over and careening down her cheeks where he'd see them, if not taste them in her kiss.

Dammit. Why couldn't she just enjoy the time they did have together, rather than ruining it while thinking about his leaving?

He pulled back just far enough to say, "Don't cry."

Too late to hide it now. She drew in a stuttering gasp. "I'm sorry."

"No." Thom shook his head. "Don't be sorry."

He didn't give her opportunity to say anything else as his mouth covered hers in a need-filled kiss.

It had been months since they'd stood in the same room. Just as long since they'd sated their need for each other.

Her body won the tug of war for dominance with her mind and she was happy for that. She hated that her anticipation of the pain of Thom leaving so often robbed her of the enjoyment of the short time she had him there.

Obviously, she was deranged and incapable of even enjoying—

Thom lifted her and tossed her onto the mattress, following her down and pushing all thought from her mind as his body covered hers.

"Damn, I missed you." His kiss became more demanding as he snaked his hand beneath the waistband of her pajama bottoms.

He groaned as his hand connected with her bare skin. Pushing up and off her with both arms he sat up on his knees and tugged the bottoms down her legs.

"Don't ever start wearing underwear, okay?" His eyes appeared out of focus as he began to strip her.

"Okay," she agreed, rather than tell him she'd never actually leave the house without putting on underwear. Since she was in pajama bottoms and at home most of the time, it didn't seem important to discuss it any further.

As Thom leaned low and she felt the heat of his mouth between her thighs, she decided she'd probably do whatever he asked of her anyway. Including forego panties in public, propriety be damned.

Things always moved fast when they'd been apart for a while. Between his mouth and his hands on her, she was gasping in moments. Shaking as her muscles tensed and the climax broke over her body that had been too long denied.

She was still throbbing with aftershocks when Thom climbed off the bed and started flinging off his clothes. Then he was on top of her, his lean muscles and rock hard body feeling as perfect as ever beneath her hands. She held on with both hands, gripping his strong arms, anchoring herself, body and mind as he plunged inside.

He gasped as he moved, "I'm not gonna last."

"It's okay." She didn't know how long they had together, but she assumed it was long enough to do this again, at least once.

Breathing hard, he sped his stroke, held deep and shuddered.

Collapsing, he rolled to one side before his weight crushed her. He flopped back onto the pillow and threw one forearm over his face. "Damn. I'm sorry. I couldn't hold on any longer."

"It's fine." She moved closer so their legs

touched, just happy he was there with her. In the same country. In the same state. In the same bed. It was all more than they'd had recently. "I've got nowhere else to be. We can do it again."

"Oh, we're definitely gonna do that again," he said, laughing.

She took advantage of the opportunity to escape to the bathroom to get cleaned up while Thom lay, still fighting to regain his breath. Ginny swung her legs over the other side of the bed and slipped off to the bathroom.

In private, she washed away the dried tears from her face and swiped on some quick light makeup. The natural look was one thing, but she saw him too infrequently to completely abandon putting on at least a bit when he was around.

She pulled on a robe before going back out, where she found Thom watching her from the bed, right where she'd left him.

Feeling nostalgic and vulnerable again, she tried to memorize the look of him there so she could revisit it when he was gone again.

All that thought did was make the tears threaten to emerge again.

Thom frowned. "You still look sad. What's wrong, baby?"

"I don't want to ruin your visit. Let's not talk about it."

"No." He pinned her with his stare. "That's not how this works. We're a team."

"Yeah? What's our name? SEAL Team 2 for the two of us?" She joked to lighten the mood, without much luck.

"Uh, no. There's already one of those. Come on. Tell me. What's wrong?"

"I miss you already." The tears really let loose at the admission, in spite of his smile.

He reached for her, grasping her hand in his and pulling her closer. "But I'm right here."

"You won't be for long. You'll have to leave again." She let him pull her to the bed and kneeled on the edge of the mattress.

Thom locked his gaze on hers. "I know. Things have been particularly crazy lately. It's Ramadan."

"What?" she asked, confused.

He shook his head. "Nothing for you to worry about, but I swear to you, usually I spend seventy-five percent of the time training and a lot of that happens right in Virginia."

"But I'm not in Virginia. I'm here."

"Yeah. That's kind of what I came here to talk to you about. About changing that. Soon, I hope."

Heart pounding, Ginny listened to his words. What was he saying?

"How is that going to change?" she asked, breathless.

Thom blew out a huff of air and said, "I guess this is as good a time as any."

He dropped his hold on her and got out of bed. He walked, barefoot and naked, to the jumble of clothes on the floor.

After pulling on his underwear, he bent to grab the jeans he'd dropped. He felt in the pocket as he said, "I had been hoping to a least have on pants when I did this but . . ."

Through her tears, she watched him pull a ring

box out of the pocket of the jeans in his hands. It was like standing indoors and trying to see outside through a rain drenched window. Everything appeared wavy and watery as he got down on one knee and flipped open the box.

She dashed away the tears with both hands and tried to get a clearer view because inside that box was a thin gold band featuring a single sparkling diamond.

"Will you marry me?" As he stared up at her holding that ring, her dark haired warrior, the man she loved to the point of pain, there was nothing in the world she wanted more.

There was also no way to control the tears that fell anew.

She nodded until her curls tumbled across her eyes. Blowing the hair out of the way she swiped at her tears again.

"Is that a yes?" he asked with a smile.

"Yes."

"Good." Thom stood.

He stepped closer and took her hand. His larger one warmed hers as he slid the ring onto her finger. She felt the tremble in his hands, or maybe it was her who was shaking.

She didn't have much time to think more about it as Thom's eyes narrowed and he pressed closer, cradling her face in his hands.

"Come here, soon to be wife." He kissed her as if it were the first time, but at the same time with a familiarity that came from years of loving each other.

"Are we heading back to bed?" she asked,

through the kiss.

"Mm, hm." His response was muffled by her mouth.

She didn't argue. There was nothing she wanted more than spending every second with Thom. It didn't matter what they did—eat, walk, snuggle on the sofa in front of the TV. . . If she was touching him, even better. And if he was naked?

Yeah, that proofreading job was going to have to wait. So was everything else on her schedule.

He was hard again. She felt him pressing against her as he backed her toward the bed, sliding the robe off her shoulders at the same time. "You might as well stop putting your clothes back on. I'm just gonna take them off again."

"You put on your underwear," she pointed out.

"Thanks for reminding me." He pushed the offending item down his legs and kicked until they went flying to the floor. "There."

Wrapping his arms around her until she was captive in his embrace, he tumbled them both to the bed. He was over her, pressing her into the mattress with his weight, his muscles flexing beneath her hands as she wrapped her arms around his back.

She clung to him as he moved and felt her body react to his, tightening, poised for release.

Running her hands down, she pulled him in tighter, closer against her and cried out with the orgasm that hit.

A tremble ran through him as he moved, slow and deep, as her body gripped his until her spasms slowed. Then Thom's stroke sped.

He loved her fast and hard until she felt him

straining above her. He drove into her with one final stroke and groaned before he collapsed on top of her.

It was a while before he rolled off her, but she didn't mind. She'd happily be crushed by him. But when she was free she extricated her hand from the tangle of bedding and stared down at the strange sight of the ring on her finger.

He angled his head on the pillow to glance her direction and laughed. "You know, I was a little worried about asking you."

Bracing his head on his hand as he propped up on one elbow, Thom reached out to take hold of her left hand. He ran his thumb over the ring.

"Really?" Ginny frowned. "Why?"

He lifted one shoulder. "I was afraid you'd had it with all the bullshit. With the travel and me canceling on you all the time. I was afraid that you were tired of it all and me."

"No. I love you too much. I'd never get tired of you." She shook her head, baffled that he could possibly not realize how much she loved him. How much she wanted to be with him all the time.

And now she would be. That fact still hadn't settled in yet.

He drew in a deep breath and let it out slowly. "That's good, because there's something I have to tell you."

Uh, oh. By the look on his face and the tone of his voice, she guessed she wasn't going to like it.

CHAPTER EIGHT

"It looks like we can apply for the license today. Thirty bucks. Bargain." Thom leaned closer to the screen. "Fun fact, if we get the license today we can legally get married tomorrow."

With hair still damp from his post-sex shower and dressed in nothing but a pair of U.S. NAVY shorts, he looked yummy and right at home on Ginny's sofa. She wouldn't mind if he was on it a whole lot more often.

He was going away again soon, he'd already told her that, even though he wouldn't say exactly when or to where, but they had until Sunday night. That was still days away. Days they didn't even have to leave this room if they didn't want to.

Thom looked up from the laptop. "Ginny?"

"Hmm?" Cradling her tea mug in both hands and thinking more about his muscles than his words she forced her attention to what he was saying.

He smiled. "What have you got in that mug? You celebrating our engagement with a drink without me?"

She walked to the sofa. Perched on the edge, she tried to pull the sides of her robe closer to her legs with one hand. "Just tea. What did you say before?"

"I said, if we get moving and can make it to the," he referred to the screen, "Stamford Government Center on Washington Boulevard before fifteen-thirty today we can get our license."

Stupid military time. Narrowing her eyes as she concentrated, Ginny was just doing the math and subtracting twelve from fifteen in her head when Thom smirked.

"That's three-thirty."

"Oh, okay. Thanks." Annoyed he'd caught her figuring it out with her shitty math skills she scowled, until she realized what he was saying. "Wait, today? Why?

"There's a one day delay between getting the license and getting married. Doesn't it make sense to have it in our hands so we can do it whenever we want?"

"Yeah. Does it expire though?"

He shook his head. "Not for sixty-five days."

"Sixty-five days?" she squeaked.

"That's two months, plus a couple of days."

She frowned at him. "I know. I can do that math. Just not stupid military time. But that's so soon. You want to get married within the next two months?"

"Yes. I'd get married tomorrow if you wanted, but definitely after I get back from this next assignment. The sooner, the better. Don't you want that too?"

"I do. I want to *be* married to you, more than anything in the world. I'm just not sure I want to *get* married that fast."

He stared at her with a blank expression that told Ginny he didn't grasp the nuance.

"I'm saying, how are we going to put together a wedding in that short of a time."

"The Justice of the Peace can probably do it on a couple of days notice." Watching her reaction to his statement, Thom let out a breath. "And you hate that idea."

"No. Not really." Visions of her dream wedding with the white dress and pink bridal bouquet and blue hydrangea table centerpieces danced in her head before being pushed aside by the image of a cold, sterile municipal building office.

"Yes, you do." Thom put the laptop on the coffee table and wrapped his hands around her waist to tug her closer. "We'll have whatever kind of wedding you want. Whenever you want it. Just be aware, my savings account is pretty much depleted right now so let's not go too crazy since I have yet to figure out how I'm going to pay for it."

"I have some savings put aside." As he scowled at her offer she added, "And I don't want anything big anyway. Just simple and small. I just never considered the Justice of the Peace. The idea took me by surprise, but you know what? Now that I think about it, it might not be that bad."

As she warmed to the concept, the steady shake of Thom's head robbed her of her new found excitement for the plan.

"What's wrong?" she asked.

"I don't want you to regret not having the wedding you want."

"I won't." She could still wear a pretty dress and carry a bouquet. Molly could still be her maid of honor. And they could still have a small party afterward to celebrate with close friends and family. Thoughts of family let to thoughts of her mother. Shit. That was the one wrench in this quickie wedding plan. Her shoulders slumped at the thought. "My mother might though."

He dipped his head in a nod. "Yup. She might."

"It's our wedding. Not hers." She frowned in protest.

"And you're her only daughter."

Ginny sighed. Now that he was tossing obstacles in the way of their getting married sooner rather than later, it made her want it even more. She began to form a plan.

"How about we get the license today so we have it and then we can decide later. You said it's only thirty dollars. So if it expires, we'll just get another one." She caught a glimpse at the clock. "Oh my God. If they close at three-thirty I'd better get dressed so we can leave."

"We have time."

Already up and across the tiny apartment, she didn't even slow down in her barefoot sprint to the closet as she called back, "No. There'll be traffic. Get dressed."

Thom snorted. "Because I'm the one it takes so long to get ready?"

She leaned around the bedroom screen. "Brat. Be nice to me or I'll tell my mother you're the one who talked me into a quickie wedding at the Justice of the Peace."

Thom cringed. "Please don't."

She laughed and went back to deciding what to wear to get her marriage license. Then she realized that was the least of her worries.

What was she going to wear to get married? She'd need a dress. And shoes. And how would she wear her hair? Up or down? Her mind spun with all the decisions.

Married. Holy cow. Never mind the logistics of the actual ceremony to get them married, the whole idea in general was pretty overwhelming.

As she slid off her robe and stood in front of her closet naked, she marveled at the sudden and wonderful changes in her life.

She'd gone from dating and wondering if they'd ever get married, to being engaged.

It wasn't exactly as she'd imagined it would happen, with him having to leave again so soon and her doing the planning mostly on her own, but that was fine. Becoming Mrs. Thomas Grande would be worth it.

Though maybe she'd be Virginia Starr-Grande instead.

That had a nice ring to it. And it would make a pretty kick ass pen name to write under too when she finally got a book of her own actually published.

Glancing up, she saw Thom leaning against the wall and watching her. There was a glint of desire in his eyes as his gaze took in her nakedness.

"We don't have time for that," she warned, knowing exactly what was on his mind.

His lips twitched with a smile. "There's always time for that."

"No. It's almost two," she warned. "We need to be there before three-thirty."

"Plenty of time." As he closed the distance between them and wrapped his hands around her waist she knew she was losing this debate.

The warmth of his rough palms against her bare skin sent a tingle through her. Maybe they did have a little bit of time to spare . . . "Okay, but we can't take too long."

Raising a brow, he laughed. "I'll do my best."

Lifting her, he tossed her naked onto the bed where she was happy to watch him pull off what little clothing he had on.

He was quick to strip out of the shorts and T-shirt, and then he was crawling on the bed, pushing her legs wider with his hands as he moved between them.

"Are you still going to be so insatiable when we're married?"

He sniffed out a laugh as he gazed up at her from his spot between her thighs. "What do you think?"

As he dipped his head and she felt the heat of his tongue hit her, eliciting a moan from her throat, she had a feeling she had nothing to worry about in that department.

CHAPTER NINE

Sunday came and Thom left, just as Ginny knew he had to, but this time felt different.

This time it was her soon-to-be-husband who left her with the promise they'd talk more about the wedding as soon as possible. She'd be handling a lot of the details on her own, without him even accessible by phone at times, but then again they never did have a normal relationship.

Crazy woman that she was, maybe that's the part she loved most.

She was engaged. They were engaged. Ginny repeated the words in her head. It didn't quite feel real yet there alone in her apartment with no one to share the joy with, not even a cat. She had to tell someone or she was going to bust.

That she'd avoided talking to anyone for the few days Thom had been there had been a miracle but now he was gone and she was alone and antsy.

Standing in the middle of the room with the phone in her hand, she felt about to crawl out of her skin if she didn't tell somebody, but whom did she call first? Her best friend or her parents?

An incoming call kicked her into action. One glance at the display told her that her decision of whom to speak with first had been made for her.

She answered and pressed the device to her ear. "Mom. Hi."

"Hi. I'm just calling to ask whether you're going to see your father for Father's Day or will you be *traveling*?" The vitriol in her mother's tone had Ginny's hair standing on end.

Now was obviously not the time to tell her mother anything to do with Thom.

The amount of time she spent with him was already a sore topic. What would the reaction be to the news of her marrying him and moving to Virginia?

She didn't want any negativity spoiling her brand new engaged happiness. The only way to insure that was to keep the news to herself for now. She probably shouldn't even tell Molly. Ginny knew her friend spoke to her mother, more than was normal, in Ginny's opinion. Molly might slip and tell.

No, keeping it quiet for now seemed safest.

"No, no traveling. I'll be around for Father's Day."

"Fine. I'm cooking his favorite for dinner if you want to come over." The attitude was still there, shadowing every word.

Stifling a sigh, Ginny said, "I'll make a

cheesecake for dessert, if you want."

"All right. That would be good. He likes that." That last response had sounded almost normal instead of icy.

The pastry peace offering had worked. Crisis averted . . . for now. At least until she brought up the engagement.

Deciding to test the waters and see what she was in for when she did drop the bomb, Ginny said, "You know, Mom, one day Thom and I might decide to, I don't know, move in together or get married. And then you're going to have to be okay with me visiting less and missing some holidays."

"You've been dating for years. If he was going to propose he would have done it already."

"It hasn't been that long—"

"And," Ginny's mother continued, cutting her off, "*if* that ever happened, he can just move up here to live. His parents live up here too. Correct?"

"Yes. In Massachusetts."

"Well, then it's ridiculous for him to live so far away down there in Virginia in the first place. He can move."

"But he's in the Navy—"

"So? There's that base in New London he can work at. I see the signs for it when we drive by on the way to that outlet center I like."

Ginny opened her mouth to list all the reasons Thom lived where he did, but then closed it again. There was no arguing with a woman as stubborn and close-minded as her mother.

She was beginning to understand why Romeo 1 Juliet had chosen to keep their marriage a secret. In fact, eloping was looking pretty good right about now.

Ginny sighed. Yup. No way was she bringing up the engagement today.

Hopefully Thom was going to have better luck telling the kids about their plan to get married.

Kids. The word set her heart pounding. Of course she knew Thom had a son and a daughter, but what that truly meant to her once they were married hadn't really hit her until right this moment.

Ginny was going to be a *stepmother*.

Did that make her own mom and dad step-grandparents? And how was that news going to go over?

She was a bit afraid to find out.

CHAPTER TEN

Thom stood outside the door of the house where he used to live—the one he still paid the bills for—and steeled himself with a bracing breath as he rang the bell.

When the woman he'd once loved, many years ago, opened the door he glanced up and said, "Hi."

Her expression changed to one of annoyance the moment she saw him. Folding her arms across her chest, she said, "You can't just show up to see the kids whenever you want—"

"I'm not here to see the kids. I wanted to talk to you." Though since the kids were out of school for summer break they should be home and if she weren't such a bitch, she'd let him see them even if it wasn't his planned day to do so.

She screwed her mouth up tighter. "If you're ↑ about the support payments I'm telling you now that I can't afford to live on any less money and raise your children—"

"Debbie, this isn't about money."

"What then?" She cocked a brow expectantly, as if it was too much work for her to wait for him to finish up what he had to say and leave.

Jeez, it wasn't like they'd been married for years and had two children together or anything.

He resisted the urge to roll is eyes at that thought and instead said, "Can I come in?"

"I guess so." She took a single step back from the doorway.

How magnanimous of her, letting him in the house he still paid for. Pressing his lips together to keep from blowing up at her he silently stepped past her and into the foyer. He turned back as she closed the door and faced him.

"Well?" she asked. "You want to talk? Talk. Why are you here?"

He glanced into the living room. The fact there was some daytime talk show on the television and not cartoons prompted him to ask, "The kids here?"

"Nope."

Frowning, he asked, "Where are they?"

"Play date." She crossed her arms again, as if challenging him to dispute her. Or maybe she was just as tired of talking to him as he was of talking to her.

No shock there. The only shocker was that they'd been happy together at all once upon a time.

Time to wrap up this visit and cut to the chase. "I'm getting remarried."

Her eyes widened before they narrowed. Debbie never could hide her feelings from him, not that she ever really tried. "That woman you've been dating?"

"Ginny." He'd been with *that woman* for long enough, Debbie damn well knew her name, but he supplied it anyway.

"When?"

"I'm not sure yet. She's going to try to plan it around my deployments."

She let out a sniff. "Good luck with that."

Thom knew the last thing Debbie wished Ginny was good luck, but that wasn't the point of his telling her in the first place. His children were. "It's going to be up north since that's where both our parents live. I want the kids there."

Debbie cocked a brow. "That's going to be very inconvenient."

Inconvenient? What the hell? She wasn't seriously going to deny him his kids for his wedding day, was she? He wouldn't put it past her.

He sighed. "Why?"

"What if they're in school?"

"We'll plan it during the school break."

"How will they get there? Who will supervise them? Surely you don't expect me to bring them."

He let out a short bitter laugh at that idea. Having his ex-wife anywhere near Ginny was the last thing he wanted. "No, I don't. I'll drive them up and back."

She glared at him. "And who's going to watch them when you're busy with her?"

"My mother and father are perfectly capable of taking care of their own grandchildren." The grandchildren they didn't see nearly often enough because of this very attitude Debbie was throwing at him now.

It would be nice if Juliette and Jason could have an extended visit with their grandparents in Massachusetts. Besides, how much would it suck to have to rush back to Virginia right after the wedding if Debbie decided to play hardball and not let him have them for more than the weekend?

If that happened maybe he could ask one of the guys to bring the kids back to Virginia right after the wedding. Brody's brother Chris Cassidy was retired from the teams so he had time. It was a lot to ask, but Chris had known the kids since the day they were born.

That didn't mean Debbie would agree to any of it.

She let out a huff. "We'll see."

Barely contained anger seethed within him. Clenching his jaw until his teeth ached, he breathed in through his nose and tried to not say all the things he was thinking.

"Just let me know when," Debbie added. She must have noticed his expression and interpreted his angry reaction correctly so decided to play nice.

"Fine. I will." He moved toward the door when she reached out a hand to stop him.

He glanced at her grip on his arm and then up to her face. He cocked a brow in question.

"If you're planning on trying to see the kids this week, you have to let me know in advance. I have plans."

"You have plans?" he asked. *Plans* as in a date?

If she was trying to make him jealous, it wasn't

going to work. He couldn't care less who she went out with. God willing she'd get remarried and be someone else's problem, although who knew what kind of guy she would choose? That was definitely his concern since that man would be in his kids' lives.

More importantly, if she had plans, then why didn't she let him babysit them for the night?

He knew the answer to that without asking. Because the unpredictable nature of his job made him probably the most unreliable babysitter around.

Maybe he bore more of the responsibility for her bad attitude than he was willing to admit.

She shook her head. "I should have said *they* have plans. There's a sleepover Wednesday night. And a pool party on Saturday. And Juliette is taking a summer dance class and Jason has intramural—"

"I got it." He held up a hand to stop her list. He didn't need the rundown. The kids' schedules were crazy and he knew it and Debbie bore the brunt of driving them around. "I'll let you know as early as I can."

"Okay." Hoping that was the last word from her, he reached for the knob. This time he actually got to turn it without her stopping him with more conversation. With a quick glance back, Thom said, "I'll call you."

She nodded and then, thankfully, he was free.

It was like a cloud of bad vibes and toxic air had lifted the moment she closed the front door after him. Though the weight of his annoyance and simmering anger over her resistance to the kids coming to the wedding remained.

He needed a distraction and he wasn't going to find it in the room in the bachelor barracks he currently called home.

Sliding the cell out of his pants pocket as he strode toward the SUV, Thom decided some guy time with his buddies might be in order. He'd been out of touch with the real world while at Ginny's, which had suited him just fine, but he was pretty sure the NBA playoffs were on TV this week.

Scrolling through his contacts, he hit the screen to call Brody. When his friend answered, Thom asked, "You busy?"

"Nope. Just home chilling. What's up with you?"

"I just left the ex-wife."

Brody blew out a laugh. "I'm sorry. You need a drink?"

"As a matter of fact, yeah. I do. You mind if I stop by? Or we can go out if you want." As long as he could get a cold beer and some distraction, he didn't care where he was. Usually Brody felt the same.

"Come on over. I'll have a cold one waiting on you when you get here."

His friend knew him so well.

"Appreciate it. See you in a few." Thom disconnected the call and climbed into the SUV.

Turning onto the main road, he headed for Brody's apartment and a hopefully mind-erasing beer that would help him forget the shitty visit with the ex.

CHAPTER ELEVEN

"Hello, my soon-to-be-bride."

Ginny smiled at the sound of Thom's voice through the cell phone. "Hello, my soon-to-be-groom."

"I just wanted to say goodnight."

"Mmm. That's nice. Thank you." She snuggled deeper beneath the covers, cradling the cell between her head and the pillow. "So what did you do today?"

"I stopped by the house after work."

The house was what he called where his ex-wife and children lived.

She tamped down the jealousy that his ex was in town with him and could see him any time she wanted, while Ginny was hundreds of miles away and barely saw him at all.

That was going to change soon. She had to remember that. "Did you tell the kids about us?" she asked.

"No. I haven't told the kids yet."

"Why not?" Was he afraid they wouldn't accept her?

That renewed her worry about the whole stepmother thing she'd managed to forget about in favor of the other big concern—telling her mother.

"I stopped by but they were at a play date. I haven't arranged a time to see them yet, but I told Debbie."

"You did? Wow. And?" she asked.

"She was . . . fine with it."

"Oh? Good. I'm glad." Though what Ginny would really be glad about was when *she* was his wife and living down there with him.

His sixty days from license to marriage plan looked better by the second.

"You sound sleepy. Did I wake you?" Thom asked.

"Nope. Just in bed watching TV."

"There's not going to be television watching in the bed once you get your sweet self down here after we're married."

Ginny cringed at his pronouncement, keeping to herself that her favorite thing to do in bed—aside from sex—was to watch television. But less than a week into their secret engaged life, she didn't feel the need to argue the point long distance.

Instead, she joked, "Promises, promises."

"Nope. Just the truth. So did you tell your parents yet that we're engaged?"

"Um, no."

"Did you at least tell Molly?"

"Um. No . . ."

"I thought you were excited about this wedding."

"I am, I'm just afraid some people might have another opinion."

He sighed. "Your mom."

"Yes."

"Okay, take what time you need. But I'm warning you, if you don't get this thing planned for soon I might just start

trying to commute from Connecticut to Virginia."

"Could you do that?"

Thom snorted. "A seven-hour drive each way? Uh, no. I was just joking."

She rolled her eyes. "I know you couldn't really commute, but I thought maybe you could, I don't know, get like firemen hours? You know, two days on, three days off. Or something like that."

He laughed. "That would be very nice but the Navy doesn't exactly work like that. And actually . . ."

Crap. She was starting to dread his long pauses. Nothing good ever followed. She braced herself for the inevitable.

". . . it looks like I might be, um, *busy* at work much sooner than I thought. And communications might be spotty for a while here and there when I'm *traveling*."

Busy. Traveling. Yeah, sure. She smothered a snort, knowing it was all euphemisms for him going away to someplace dangerous to do something deadly.

"When I'm in the same room with you, in the same house, on the base where they sweep for bugs and know that we're secure from spies, are you going to actually tell me stuff? Or will we still speak in code like this?" she asked.

"Well, first of all, they don't *sweep for bugs,* as you put it, in base housing. At least, not as far as I know. But yeah, we'll be able to talk a little more freely than we can now on the phone. Within reason, of course."

Within reason. Meaning he'd still keep things from her, but at least she'd be there with him when he did it. That would have to be good enough. "Okay."

"Are you really? Okay, I mean?" he asked.

"You're not here, so I'm not exactly the happiest newly engaged girl in Connecticut, but I'll be all right. Just make sure you come back to me. And in time for the wedding—whenever that is."

He laughed. "Yeah, about that. Can you get working on that soon—setting a wedding date—so I have some idea when to beg for leave? Please?"

The dreaded task of telling her mother she was moving away hung like a dark cloud blocking the sunshine of her pending marital bliss. But she'd need to do that before she could choose a date. "I'll take care of it. I promise."

"Can I believe you?" he asked, with humor in his tone.

Ginny drew her brows low. "Yes. Why wouldn't you?"

"We might be apart a lot, but I know you. You would procrastinate breathing if you could get away with it."

Her frown deepened but knowing it was true she

couldn't deny his accusation. She could only be insulted by it. "You're supposed to be charmed by my little quirks."

"Oh, I am. Believe me. Completely charmed and in love with you. But right now, I'm going to say good night. I've got an early morning tomorrow."

"Okay. I love you," she said.

"And I love you. With all my heart. Remember that." His words sounded a little too final. As if this might be the last time they talked for a while—or ever.

Ginny swallowed hard. "I remember."

"Oh, and if you aimed for a weekend close to a full moon for the wedding, that would be good."

She lifted her brows at that strange request. "A full moon?"

"Yup. Just a suggestion." He was being vague, skirting the issue, which only made Ginny more determined to know.

"Um, okay. I'll look into that." As well as why he might be requesting a full moon for their wedding, because she was fairly certain it wasn't because he thought it would be romantic and pretty for the pictures.

If she hadn't been the queen of internet research before, dating Thom, with all of his secrets, had made her one.

"Good. All right. Let me go. If I don't get in touch with you tomorrow, I will as soon as I can. Okay?"

Swallowing the lump of dread from her throat, Ginny said, "Okay."

"Good night, baby."

"Good night." Tears filled her eyes when she heard the call go dead. She missed him constantly and worried about him already even if he hadn't left the country yet.

The sooner she moved to be with him the better and to do that she needed to suck it up and face the music—or more accurately, face the parents.

Bracing herself, Ginny decided to do that tomorrow and to make sure she didn't chicken out she would set up a time to see them right now.

She glanced at the clock. It was probably too late to call but she could email. She grabbed her laptop off the coffee table. Her email inbox was open, as usual, so she tapped out a quick message to her mother asking if she could come over for lunch tomorrow and then hit SEND before she could change her mind.

One down, one to go. Drawing in a deep breath, she picked up the cell and typed in a quick text to Molly.

I have news. Call me when you can.

When a reply didn't come back in seconds—which it would have if Molly had been awake—Ginny let out the breath she'd been holding.

She was about to put down the cell when a brilliant idea struck. She typed in a second text to Molly.

Can you have lunch with me tomorrow?

Having Molly there would be a good buffer. The woman took a long lunch every day to go shopping. She could darn well spend it with Ginny instead when her friend needed her.

Tomorrow, for better or worse, she'd be a

publicly engaged woman. And hopefully it wouldn't be too much longer before she'd be a married one as well.

Which reminded her . . . grabbing her laptop again she opened a new browser tab and typed into the search bar "calendar of moon phases".

She'd get the dates of the full moon first, and then she was going to move on to trying to find the reason behind Thom's odd request, even if it took her all night.

CHAPTER TWELVE

"So he just asked you to marry him and then left?" The judgment was clear in Molly's tone, even through the cell phone.

Temper rising, Ginny was starting to regret telling her best friend about what should be the happiest moment of her life. "No. He was here for four days. He stayed until late Sunday when he had to leave for Virginia to get back to the base."

Molly sucked in a breath. "He was here all that time, and proposed, and you never called me so we could go out and celebrate?"

That was exactly why Ginny hadn't told Molly while Thom was still there. Their time together was too limited, too precious, to spend it out at some crowded bar or restaurant.

All in all, Molly's reaction so far to the news of the engagement didn't bode well for the upcoming revelation with her parents later that day. Ginny had thought Molly would be the easier of the two, but it wasn't turning out that way.

"We wanted to be alone. I'm sorry I didn't call you, I really am, but we have so little time together. And you're supposed to be happy for me. You're my best friend and I just got engaged."

"I know. And I am. Really. I'm just feeling left out."

Ginny sniffed out a laugh. "You won't be left out for long. I'm going to need help. We want to have the wedding as soon as possible."

She was armed and ready with a list of upcoming weekends near full moons.

"How soon is soon?" Molly asked.

"Like this summer."

"You do realize it's already June, right?"

"I know. And it might not work but I'd like to try."

"What's the rush—" Molly sucked in a breath. "Oh my God. You're pregnant!"

Ginny shook her head. "No, I'm not. Thom has a vasectomy."

"Oh. Eww. Too much information, thank you very much. Change of subject, have you discussed where you're going to live?"

"Yes, of course. We'll live in Virginia."

"Oh, boy. Your mother is going to freak out. I'm not too happy about it either, but your mom—"

"I know." Ginny didn't need to hear it from Molly. She already knew the move was not going to go over well. "It can't be helped. He has to be near his base."

"He can't get a transfer to another base?"

"I don't think so." She hadn't asked Thom specifically but she knew his SEAL team was based in Virginia so that's where he had to be.

"Well, that sucks."

"I know, but you can come and visit me. It's beautiful down there by the water. And there are tons of Navy men." Ginny dangled that temptation in front of her single and always looking friend. Between the beaches and bars, all teeming with male eye candy, she'd manage to keep Molly occupied.

"There is that." Molly laughed. "So you haven't told your mother yet?"

"No, I'm going over today to have lunch and break it to them."

"Oh, please. Can I come?"

Ginny laughed. "Yes. Why do you think I texted asking you about lunch? But the question is why would you want to be there?"

"Well, I want to see the ring. But mostly I think it should be one hell of a show when you tell her you're moving."

Ginny glanced down at the diamond on her left hand. A perfect single solitaire on a band of white gold. Not showy, but classic. Thom had done well choosing and she wanted Molly to see it. She only hoped the ring was enough to also charm her mother into accepting the marriage.

"When and where?" Molly asked.

"Noon. My parents' house."

"All right. I can do that. What are you wearing?"

Ginny shook her head. No matter what the issue at hand was, good or bad, it always circled back to what outfit to wear with Molly.

Some days that trait could be really annoying—even best friends could have quirks that got on each other's nerves once in a while. But right now, with so much on her mind, Ginny was happy to join Molly in her concern about something simple, like clothes, for a little while.

CHAPTER THIRTEEN

"Ready?" Molly asked as they stood between their two vehicles parked in Ginny's parents' driveway.

"No." Ginny pouted and considered getting back inside her car and driving away to delay the inevitable.

She couldn't shake the feeling of impending doom over the upcoming event. She'd even hidden out to delay the whole thing.

Parked along the curb down the block, she'd waited until she saw Molly pull into her parents' driveway before she pulled up to the house herself. All because she didn't want to arrive first and be there alone with her parents. That's how much Ginny dreaded her mother's reaction to the news she was moving away.

"Come on." Molly tugged on Ginny's arm. "Procrastinating won't help anything."

"It might." Ginny dragged her feet to slow their progress toward the house and the certain guilt trip waiting for her within.

Molly rolled her eyes and forged ahead. "Your mother can't be upset with you when you come bearing both the good news of your engagement *and* food."

"Wanna bet?" Ginny wasn't so sure about that, but luckily she'd stopped by the gourmet shop and stocked up on their favorite foods anyway.

"You brought lunch. I have dessert and bridal magazines. We're good. We'll kill your parents with kindness. Your mother won't know what hit her."

Ginny let out a guttural noise of doubt. "Don't be so sure."

Her mother would know when Ginny delivered the news she was moving seven hours away. No question about that. But Molly was correct about one thing. Dragging this out wouldn't change anything in the end so she might as well get it over with.

Like ripping off a bandage. One quick painful yank . . .

The front door of the house swung open, ending any chance for Ginny to turn and run.

"Molly. It's nice to see you again." Ginny's mother kissed Molly's cheek.

"Nice to see you too, Mrs. Starr. Thanks for having me over. I picked up dessert. Cannoli from the Italian bakery." Molly held up the white bakery box tied with string.

Her eyes lit up. "Mmm. I can't wait. Thank you."

"My pleasure. I'll go put them in the kitchen." Molly smiled and sidled past Ginny's mother and into the house.

Then it was Ginny's turn. "Hi, Mom."

"Hello, Virginia."

Had her mother sounded happier to see Molly than her own daughter? Ginny stomped down that suspicion, but still vowed that next time she came over she'd be stopping to pick up cannoli herself.

"Where's Dad?" she asked when she saw past her mother and her father wasn't in his usual chair in the living room.

"He's out back trimming the hedges."

"Oh." With the hope she could soothe the ruffled feathers about to be caused by the upcoming announcement, Ginny held up the plastic bag in her own hand. "I picked up the chicken salad you like. And the pasta salad Dad likes."

"Oh, g—" When her mother's eyes went wide and her mouth hung open on the unfinished word, Ginny's mind reeled to figure out what was happening.

It took her a second to put the pieces together and realize what her mother was reacting to . . . and her own mistake. Her engagement ring was on the hand she'd thrust right in front of her mother's nose by holding up the bag of food.

"Um. Surprise. I'm engaged." She tried for a singsong, happy tone of voice, but wasn't sure she pulled it off.

Molly had reappeared behind Ginny's mom. Unseen by the older woman, Molly cringed before walking around to join the conversation. "Isn't it great, Mrs. Starr? And I love the ring. So classic. It'll never go out of style."

As her friend babbled, Ginny, still standing just inside the front door, decided she'd better get to the sofa and sit down for this.

She pushed past her mother. "Let's sit down."

"Yeah, there's so much to talk about and plan. It's so exciting." Even Molly's perpetual optimism seemed to fall flat in the face of Ginny's mother's stone-faced silence.

Ginny plopped the bag of food on the shelf in the fridge and returned to the living room to find her mother still narrow-eyed in spite of Molly's cheerful efforts.

"Where are you two going to live?" Ginny's mother asked.

Wow. Right to the heart of the matter. No tiptoeing around it.

"In Virginia?" *Dammit*. It was a definitive answer, so why had Ginny made it sound like a question?

Ginny's mother's lips formed a thin angry line. "So I'll just never see you again."

So many responses to that ridiculous accusation flew into Ginny's head she couldn't choose just one.

Luckily, Molly was faster. Her mouth was open before Ginny could form a coherent thought.

"Actually, Mrs. Starr, Ginny was telling me how she plans to come back to Connecticut whenever Thom deploys. And since she won't have her apartment up here anymore, she'll have to stay here with you, so you'll probably see her *more*. You know how often Thom's gone." Molly had lowered her voice for that last part, as if she and Ginny's mother shared a common distaste for how much her new husband would abandon her.

Since it seemed to be working, Ginny didn't fight it. She jumped on Molly's train of thought. "Would you mind if I stayed in my old room sometimes while Thom's away?"

"Of course not. I put my off-season clothes in your closet but I can move them into storage bins and you can keep some of your things here, if you want. That way they'll be here when you come and you don't have to travel with luggage."

"Good idea. It'll be so much easier to just jump on the train or plane with a small carry-on bag. She'll probably be up here more than she's down there with the amount of travel Thom does," Molly said.

"Mm, hm." Ginny's mother nodded.

Pushing aside the fact that her mother and her best friend were basically hoping her husband would be away more than he was home—God, how Ginny hoped that wasn't going to be true—she decided not to argue. The dark cloud her news had caused seemed to have lifted and Ginny wasn't about to bring it back again.

There was one thing she had to bring up though. Thom was waiting for her to text with a date so he could put in for leave before they flew off to wherever he hinted he was going.

"So I have a list of a few possible wedding dates I wanted to run by you just to make sure you don't have other plans."

"Sure. Let me get the calendar off the bulletin board. It's one of those eighteen-month calendars so we can see next year too." Her mother looked proud of her advance preparedness.

Too bad Ginny was going to have to burst her bubble that there was no way she was waiting until next year to have this wedding.

"Actually, we were hoping to have it this summer."

Her mother's eyes popped wide. "This summer?"

"Yes." Afraid of another meltdown, Ginny grasped for a way to get her mother on board with this plan. "That way Thom can add me to his health insurance. You know how much I'm paying now. Through the military, since he's active duty, once we're married my coverage will be free."

"Oh, that will save you a lot. But this summer? How will you find anywhere that's decent and not booked up already?"

"Maybe someplace will have a last minute cancellation," Molly suggested.

"True. I bet there are people who have to cancel events. Then maybe the catering hall would be willing to negotiate the price lower to fill the date."

"Exactly." Molly nodded in agreement with Ginny's mother as the two continued to hold the conversation without Ginny's involvement.

"Let me grab my reading glasses and the phone book. We can start calling and see if there's any availability. Ginny, what are those dates?" Her mother headed for the drawer where the big yellow phone book had lived for as long as she'd been alive.

Why did they even still print those things when everyone just looked up numbers online?

As her mother plopped the giant book onto the table next to a pen and pad of paper she'd pulled from the same catch all drawer, Ginny figured she had her answer. It was printed for people like her mother.

Ginny surrendered her short list of weekends to her mother and Molly, and watched as the suggestions started to fly.

The two steamrolled right over the concern Ginny raised about cost. They were married to their theory that the wedding being so soon would lower the price, while Ginny had her doubts. If anything, the places might try to charge more, thinking she was desperate and willing to pay it.

Catering halls. Restaurants. Hotels. Country Clubs. The list grew in spite of Ginny's protest until finally her mother stood and retrieved the phone.

Ginny jumped in before the calls began. "Mom. People really aren't having big elaborate weddings anymore these days."

Her mother raised one brow. "The people we know are."

She really couldn't fight her mother on that point so she tried changing tactics. "I'm very concerned these places will be too expensive. It has to be cheap enough that Thom and I can pay for it on our own. Out of our savings. I really don't want to go into debt for a wedding."

Ginny had managed to get through college without taking a huge loan like some of her friends had. She wasn't about to take on one now for a big wedding her mother wanted more than she did.

She would just be happy to be with Thom. None of the other stuff mattered.

Her mother waved away the concern. "Your father and I will pay for it."

That offer should have been a relief, but it wasn't. In fact, it was the exact opposite, because Ginny had dated Thom long enough to know the deal. That chances were good he'd get called away and she'd be sitting there with an expensive wedding that her parents had paid for and no groom.

She'd never hear the end of it. "Thank you. That's very generous, but I can't let you do that."

"Don't be silly." Her mother waved away the concern with one hand while turning on the phone with the other.

"Mom. Seriously. Listen to me. Anyplace we choose is going to have to have a really good cancelation policy because even if he takes leave, he can still get called back in. Or worse, he could not make it back in time from wherever he is." Ginny wasn't sure a wedding venue existed that would hand you the money back without some sort of penalty if you canceled last minute.

Her mother drew in a breath. "Virginia, it doesn't hurt to call and ask."

"But—" Before Ginny could finish her mother was dialing. "Mom, please make sure you ask about cancellations."

"Shh." Her mother waved at her for silence, before saying, "Hi. I'm wondering about your availability . . ."

She glanced helplessly at Molly. Her friend

shrugged, which didn't help Ginny's worry about this wedding spiraling out of her control.

Ginny's cell phone rang as she was trying to listen to what her mother was saying on the phone.

One glance at the display told her she couldn't let it go to voicemail. It was Thom.

She wanted to talk to him, but she needed to keep an eye on her mother.

It was not lost on her that not even an hour after telling her mother about the wedding she was already stressed beyond belief.

Drawing in a deep breath, she answered the call. "Hello."

"Hey, baby. We're on a short break so I thought I'd call. Since you didn't text me with a date I'm going to assume you haven't told your parents yet. Correct?"

"No. Not correct. I told everybody I was supposed to tell." Which was why she was starting to get a headache.

"Really. Wow. I'm impressed. And? How did it go?" he asked.

"Good. Really good. They're very happy for us and excited about planning the wedding."

"And they were okay with you moving to Virginia?" he asked.

"Yup. Totally fine with me moving." Ginny ignored Molly's raised brow and turned slightly on the sofa to attain some semblance of privacy.

"Good. I'm glad. You know what I'm really glad about?" he asked.

"No. What?"

"That all those dates you emailed me last night

for possible wedding weekends are so soon." There was a smile in his tone.

"Really? I was worried they were *too* soon. Are you sure you'll be back in time?"

"Sure? No." He laughed. "Nothing is certain in the military. But I talked to Grant. He thinks we should be good."

"I picked the weekends on either side of the full moons for the next couple of months. Like you asked." Why he'd asked that, she still wasn't sure.

She'd have to grill him on that one day, but not today. There was too much else going on and he probably wouldn't tell her over the phone anyway.

"I noticed. That's good. God, it'll be so good to finally officially marry you and get you down here. I'm so happy your mother is okay with the move."

"Yup. She's perfectly fine with it." The lie was slipping out easier each time Ginny told it.

"All right. I gotta get back in. You on schedule to pick that date today?"

"Yup. No problem. I'll have a definite date to you by tomorrow. I promise."

"Um, any chance you can make it tonight?" Thom asked.

This was a clue. Even with everything that was going on around her, Ginny didn't miss Thom's unspoken words. That he needed the date tonight because he'd be gone by tomorrow.

Feeling ill at the thought she said, "Okay. I'll have a date for you before I leave here today."

"Perfect. Just like you."

Ginny's heart clenched at how sweet he could be. "Aw. Thank you."

"I love you," he said in the chipper voice of a happy man who'd had one big burden lifted from his shoulders.

She fought down her guilt over lying to him. "I love you too. Text you later."

"Looking forward to it. Bye."

"Bye." She hung up and saw Molly eyeing her.

"You totally lied to him."

Ginny blew out a breath. "I know."

"Why? You're going to share the rest of your lives together. Don't you think he needs to share this too?" Molly tipped her head in the direction of the table where the phone calls continued.

Ginny shook her head. "No. I can't."

"Why not?"

Because that's not what military wives did. Because there was a good chance she wouldn't get to talk to Thom again before he left for some deadly mission in some hellhole on the other side of the world. Because the last thing she wanted was him worrying about her or this wedding when he needed to be one-hundred percent focused on getting his job done and getting back to her alive.

Besides, Ginny wasn't supposed to spread it around, even to her best friend, when she knew Thom was heading out on a mission. These things were secret. And having only dated civilian men, Molly wouldn't understand all Ginny was feeling anyway. So she made up yet another lie.

"Because I don't want to scare him away before we even get married, that's why." Ginny looked up and noticed her mother had moved to the kitchen with the phone. "Shit. What's she doing in there?"

Molly glanced toward the kitchen. "No idea."

"Come on. I gotta get in there before she books the Plaza or something."

"Oh, I'd love to get married at the Plaza." Molly got a dreamy look in her eyes.

Jeez, did no one listen to her concerns? Apparently not.

"When she hangs up from this call, we're going to eat lunch. Then we're going to distract my mother with those bridal magazines you brought."

Molly screwed up her mouth. "I don't know why we're going to bother looking at dresses. I saw those dates you wrote down. The chance of you finding one, ordering it and getting it altered and back to you in time for the dates you chose is slim to none."

"You're right." Ginny chewed on her lip. The timing was tight to try and get a traditional bridal gown.

It was so ridiculous that wedding dresses not only cost a fortune but required months to order and then months more to tailor. Why was that?

Ginny had purchased plenty of dresses over her lifetime. Taken them home right from the store and worn them that night. Why couldn't she do that for her wedding dress?

Wait. She totally could.

"I know I'm right," Molly continued. "So what are you going to do?"

Happy with her new idea, Ginny said proudly, "I'm going to buy a dress off the rack. Ooo, I wonder if I can find something white and fancy enough at Marshall's or TJ Maxx." The off-price chain stores always had designer things for like eighty percent off what they charged at the department stores.

"Your wedding dress?" As Molly's eyes widened and she visibly swayed backwards, Ginny started to fear for her friend's mental health.

"Yes, my wedding dress. Don't worry. That doesn't mean we can't still look at the bridal dresses in your magazines. Come on. It'll be fun." Grabbing Molly's arm, Ginny tugged her toward the kitchen in search of her mother before Molly passed out from the horror of it all.

With the plan for a dress set in her mind, the rest seemed to fall into place too.

Why try to negotiate good terms with someplace to have the wedding when she could have it right here? Her parents had a beautiful yard. Since retiring her father was obsessed with the landscaping and it showed.

It would be much easier than trying to find a catering hall with both availability and a liberal cancellation policy.

They could rent tables and chairs, or better yet borrow them, and order food in from someplace. Maybe even the place where she'd just picked up lunch.

It would mean some work on her part, coordinating it, organizing all the details, but there was nothing Ginny loved more than a challenge. Throwing this wedding together, in a month and at a reasonable price, was going to be just that. A challenge. She couldn't wait.

And shocking her best friend and her mother

only added to the fun.

Feeling strong now that her decision was made, Ginny stalked toward where her mother had set up camp with the phone and her list.

She was taking back control of this wedding and doing it her way, starting with choosing the date right this minute and texting it to Thom before it was too late.

Operation Backyard Wedding was under way.

CHAPTER FOURTEEN

The new moon was no more than a pale orb in the dark, star-strewn night sky as two teams of commandos landed a mile outside of the city. That afforded them the advantage of surprise.

Surprise, if even for a few seconds, was the key for a successful close quarters assault. Anyone in the home they were about to raid, located in a city they weren't supposed to be in, would never see or hear the twelve men about to infiltrate what Hamza had thought was a secure hiding place for his shit.

Maybe Hamza would be there himself.

The intel specified that he'd left the area long ago, but those tracking him had also admitted they had no idea where he was currently so . . .

Usually more of a pessimist, Thom decided to try optimism for once and hope they got to nab both the man and his hard drives. After having lost the chance to recover the kidnapped American in

Afghanistan last month, the team was due a win.

Late June in Iran could suck, with temperatures reaching into the high nineties, but at least the mile run in full gear was at night. That made for less heat for their run and less stench once they reached the city streets.

They moved like ghosts—if ghosts wore body armor. It was amazing how quietly a group of well-trained men could move even when fully kitted out, loaded down with all the gear they might possibly need for the raid.

They proceeded in formation along a predetermined route that offered the most cover and concealment, while not communicating verbally with each other unless absolutely necessary.

The state of the art comm unit in Thom's ear beneath his helmet protected him from the one hundred and six decibels of the Black Hawk that had brought them in. It also incorporated radio communications.

More importantly, the device was smart enough to distinguish between sounds. It muffled loud noises such as explosives and large artillery, and amplified quieter sounds such as footsteps and voices.

The high-tech and pricey ear cuffs allowed Thom to hear the dog barking from within a courtyard they'd just passed. Dogs could screw up an op, alerting everyone nearby to their presence. But the squad was past the courtyard so fast they'd be long gone by the time the occupants looked outside to check. The dog could have just as easily been barking at a cat for all the homeowners inside would know.

As they neared the target Bravo team, commanded by Mike Groenning, split off to the north to go around the back of the walled residence. Thom's team, commanded by Grant, moved to the south to the main entrance.

Stacking up on one side of the gate that opened into the small courtyard of the house, with Brody on the other side, Thom waited.

Rocky moved into place behind him and Dawson mirrored them by moving in behind Brody. Mack and Grant, hidden in the shadows of the wall, kept watch up and down the block.

"Bravo team in position." Will's voice came through Thom's ear cuffs.

"Alpha team in position," reported Brody, acting as point for Alpha team.

"Alpha, move in," Grant issued the command over the comm unit.

Slowly, Brody reached out one hand for the handle on the gate. When he pushed it, it didn't move. Sometimes they lucked out and their targets left their doors unlocked, saving them a whole lot of trouble. Other times, like tonight, they faced a locked door.

"South entrance is locked." Brody reported.

With the aid of the night vision goggles, Thom could see it was a heavy, decorative cast iron lock built right into the gate. With that configuration, even using the team's sledgehammer Rocky had in his pack for just this sort of situation wouldn't break the lock.

Ideally, forced entry would be the last resort.

They'd rather not use a breaching charge on either the lock or the hinges if it could be avoided. That would alert everyone in the area to their presence. A Black Hawk was in the air waiting for their exfiltration but a firefight, and before they retrieved any intel, was the last thing they needed or wanted.

"North gate is chained and padlocked. Cutting it." A few seconds later, Will said, "Bravo entering north gate."

Thank goodness for the bolt cutters one member of the team always carried. The tool routinely got them into more places than weapons and explosives, and with a lot less noise.

But now Alpha team would have to run around back and enter the way Bravo team had.

Brody moved first and the rest filed after him. They moved quickly but carefully past the neighbor's house and around to the rear entrance.

"Alpha approaching north gate." Brody announced for the benefit of the two operators from Bravo team who stood watch at the back.

With four men from Bravo team already inside the courtyard, Thom listened for any indication that they'd been discovered by the occupants of the home. None came as he moved to flank the back entrance with Brody, Dawson and Rocky.

The gate had been left standing open for them by Bravo team. The metal gate at the back entrance was less decorative than the one at the front entrance and was obviously also less secure. Thank God for that.

"Entering north gate," Brody reported their position for the benefit of Bravo team as well as the commander. Brody moved through the open gate first. "Inside the perimeter. Approaching building A."

One by one they followed Brody. The closer they got to the house, the more alert Thom became. If this were the location where Osama Bin Laden's son Hamza had stashed his most important possessions—and both the CIA and Will Weber thought it was—there could be a guard. But so far, they hadn't seen anyone at all.

Hoping this whole mission hadn't been a wild goose chase, Thom reached the house and pressed flat against the wall, melting into the shadows and becoming invisible in the dark.

Bravo team was already there waiting when he arrived. In the green glow of the night vision Thom saw Will signal for Alpha team to move in. They were too close to the house and its occupants now to risk speaking.

Brody nodded and, staying pressed against the wall to one side of the door, reached for the knob.

When it didn't budge, he shook his head. Given the amount of equipment all of them were suited up in—helmet, NVGs, ear cuffs—there wasn't much of their faces showing, but Thom saw clearly as Brody silently mouthed a curse.

From what Thom could see, the door was dead bolted from the inside so there wasn't even a lock to pick.

Will gave the signal and two men from his team trotted silently around the building to check the other door while the rest of the unit waited in silence in the dark.

When Tompkins and Fitz returned it was not with good news. With his lips pressed into an unhappy line, Tompkins shook his head.

A string of curses Thom couldn't say aloud ran through his head. Likely his thoughts were echoed by every man there.

Rocky pulled the breaching charges from his kit and moved to press them along the edge of the door.

They came prepared and could blow this thing right off its hinges but it wasn't going to be pretty or quiet and it was most definitely going to alert anyone in the house plus the neighbors.

Instead of sneaking in and out quietly, they were going to have to go in hot and fight their way back out. Things had just gotten a lot more complicated.

Blowing out a breath, Thom leaned his helmet-clad head back against the wall. For the first time he noticed what was above him. He reached out and grabbed Rocky's arm to stop him from putting in the fuse, shaking his head and indicating they should all look up before blowing the door.

There was a piece of textile—a towel or carpet or something—hanging over the sill of an open window not far above them. It was high enough there were no bars on the window but low enough they should be able to reach it without too much effort.

Grinning, Will gave Thom a thumbs up.

Dawson had the team's small, extendable ladder on his back. He set it up and had no problem reaching the edge of the window and pulling himself up and over.

Thom held his breath, braced for the sound of

Dawson in trouble.

It never came. What they all did hear was the sliding of the bolt before the door opened to reveal Dawson smiling at them from inside.

They filed in two by two, on alert and prepared for a confrontation with the occupants. Though at this hour, chances were good the entire household was asleep.

Inside, operators peeled off in two-man teams, clearing room by room. They signaled as each room on the first floor was checked and found empty of occupants.

Leaving Tompkins and Fitz downstairs to stand watch, the rest filed silently up the stairs. The two-man teams peeled off to check the rooms on the second floor.

When the Alpha and Bravo team members met back by the stairs, each one signaling they'd found no one, it was obvious they were there alone.

"First and second floor rooms are all clear," Brody reported to those still outside.

"The building's empty?" Grant's surprised question came through the comm.

"Yup," Brody answered.

"It explains why the gates were locked up so tight. They secured the house and left. Probably for vacation somewhere," Rocky suggested.

Finding the place seemingly deserted made Thom more uncomfortable than finding it guarded by armed men. He shook his head. "I don't like this."

Will huffed out a breath. "Well, I for one am not going to question it. I saw a safe in the office in the north-west corner. Let's blow it, take whatever's in there and get the hell out of here."

"*If* there's anything in there," Thom said. "Why would they leave anything here when they left?"

"Why wouldn't they? They had no idea we were coming or that anybody even knows Hamza was ever here," Will pointed out.

"I guess." Thom figured they'd soon find out either way.

"Let's do this. I don't like this any more than Thom. Fucking hairs are standing up on the back of my neck." Brody headed toward the office. Thom followed, happy somebody else was as disturbed by the empty house as he was.

Thom and the others stayed outside the room against the wall as Will went inside to put a charge and wire on the safe door.

Running to take cover before the ten-second fuse blew, Will ducked through the doorway and pressed against the hallway wall.

A low rumbling blast, a puff of smoke, and then it was over. Given the thick walls of the home, Thom doubted the neighbors even heard, or could have identified the sound even if they had.

Will didn't wait for the dust to clear before he was through the door and headed for the safe. Thom followed Brody inside while Rocky and Dawson remained in the hallway on watch.

Rubbing his hands together, Will said, "Come on, baby. Daddy needs a hard drive." He swung the door wider and squatted to peer inside. "Bingo!"

"Got something?" Thom asked.

Grinning, Will glanced over his shoulder. "Oh,

hell yeah. We got lots of somethings."

"Let's start packing everything up." Pulling a sack out of a pocket in his vest, Brody moved forward toward the desk.

"We taking everything?" Dawson asked, coming in to help carry their finds.

Will nodded. "Everything that looks at all useful. Hell, even if it doesn't, take it anyway. They'll decide if it's important or not later."

They pulled open drawers. Took the file folders inside. Even pulled the drawers all the way out and checked beneath them for anything that could be taped to the bottom. Documents. Memory chips. Thumb drives. Even an old floppy disk and an old school camera that used film. It all went into their bags.

It took them eleven minutes to get in, clear the house, gather intel and be ready to get out. Thom knew because he'd counted.

"That's it. We're heading out." Looking a lot like Santa Claus loaded down with a full sack, Brody led the way to the staircase. Unlike Santa, they weren't carrying a bag full of toys, but hopefully what they had acquired would be a worthy gift for the CIA analysts.

They descended a lot less stealthily than they'd ascended as six pairs of boots pounded on the stairs. They were going home without a shot being fired and with bags full of stuff that should make the CIA very happy.

Knowing how to handle having luck this good wasn't in Thom's wheelhouse. He didn't know how to deal with it and he sure as hell didn't trust it.

"Alpha and Bravo teams exiting building A by the north door." Through his communicator Brody updated those standing guard outside.

"We have movement on the north block," Groenning reported. "Two military age males heading north-west."

That stopped them all in their tracks inside the doorway.

"Alpha. Bravo. Hold." Grant's order came through the comm unit in Thom's ear.

Shit. He knew it. No way they'd get out of this so easily.

There was no sound except for the breathing of the men surrounding him, but even that seemed to echo loudly off the walls.

Seconds ticked by, then minutes.

Finally, Groenning gave the all clear for the north-east quadrant, echoed by Clyde for the north-west quadrant.

"South-east quadrant clear," Mack reported.

"South-west also clear. Alpha, Bravo, move out," Grant ordered.

By the time they reached the street, keeping close to the wall of the property, Groenning and Clyde had joined Grant and Mack.

Grant led them back the way they'd come.

They were out of the house but not in the clear yet. They had to get to the landing zone outside of town and meet the Black Hawk for their exfiltration.

Any number of things could go wrong on their way out of the residential area of the city to the more deserted location they'd chosen for their pickup.

Thom forced himself to not review each and every thing that could go wrong and instead focused on his surroundings. Shadows in the street. The sounds of the night. The risk that could be waiting around every corner.

It wasn't until they were outside of the city limits that he started to believe their luck might actually be as good as it seemed.

A mile outside of town, they reached the landing zone. Grant painted the area with an IR laser, invisible to the naked eye but clearly marking their location for the Black Hawk crew.

But even while they stood waiting for the helo on the way to get them out, Thom couldn't seem to stand still.

"What's your problem?" Brody asked. "Your leave's approved to start for when we get back. You get to go home to your girl and get married."

That was exactly the problem. There were no problems. Things were going too smoothly.

He'd be home in plenty of time for the wedding. With time to spare even. Yet there was a feeling in his gut he couldn't ignore. An instinct that told him not to let his guard down. Some ancient internal failsafe, warning him of impending danger. It wasn't logical but he couldn't ignore it.

"I know. It's just nerves, I guess." Thom dismissed the feeling to Brody, but he knew he wouldn't be able to shake it easily.

"Hey, what weekend is this wedding?" Rocky asked.

"Two weeks, right?" Brody answered for him.

Thom nodded. "Yeah."

"If we can get a couple of weekend liberties approved, you wanna go?" Rocky asked Brody.

"Sure." He cut his gaze to Thom. "That a'ight?"

"Of course. I want you guys there. Ginny sent out the invites. They'll be waiting for everyone when we get back."

"Hey, you know what?" Rocky said. "If we can get a couple of extra days leave approved, we could go to my family's cabin in Pennsylvania for your bachelor party. It's nothing fancy. Generator. Outhouse. But it's beautiful up there. A creek for fishing. Woods for hunting."

Thom considered that. "Ginny might actually approve of a bachelor party like that. Yeah. If you guys can swing getting away, that would be cool. Thanks."

"No problem." Rocky grinned.

"And if we can't get leave, we'll just take you to the strip club for a night out before you head up north." Brody smiled.

"Yeah, that Ginny would definitely not approve of." Thom laughed, feeling lighter as the ominous warning bells in his head were drowned out by the sound of the Black Hawk coming to get them the hell out of there.

Next stop, the support base at Ashgabat in Turkmenistan. From there they'd slowly work their way home. But even with as slow as the military worked at times, it shouldn't take them two weeks to hit Virginia. No where near it. Not at this time of year.

He ducked beneath the rotor wash and boarded

their ride out of town.

With any luck he'd be in Connecticut with plenty of time to spare . . . and just thinking that had Thom fearing he'd jinxed him and Ginny both. In fact, he wasn't going to let himself relax and stop worrying until his feet were in her apartment in Stamford.

He looked around for some wood to knock to reverse the jinx and, of course, didn't find any. That didn't make him feel any more confident.

Crap.

CHAPTER FIFTEEN

Ginny cradled the cell on one shoulder after she tried and failed at folding laundry one handed. "Mom, this shower you're planning is getting a little crazy."

"Virginia, we're doing everything you wanted for the wedding, no matter how ridiculous it was. But Molly and I are doing what *we* want for your shower."

"But—"

"Stop. Thom isn't involved in the bridal shower. Only you are. And you're here so we don't have to worry about cancellation policies, do we?"

"No." Ginny couldn't argue that point.

"And I'm paying for the shower so you can't complain about the cost."

"But I don't want you to spend all your money just for a party for me."

"I want to spend my money on a party for you.

You're my only daughter and hopefully, unlike Thom, you'll only be getting married once in your life. Right?"

Ginny drew in a breath at that loaded question. "Yes."

"Then let me do this for you."

"Okay. Thank you." She stifled a sigh and tried to be grateful.

"So, I met with the manager at The Venetian and we went over the menu for the shower. He can definitely do a chocolate fountain—"

As her mother rambled on about the menu, Ginny's mind wandered. Maybe The Venetian Hall wouldn't be as bad on the inside as it was on the outside. She could only hope, because the outside was pretty gaudy. Gold lions sat high on columns flanking the drive, which was through the tall golden filigree gates.

Didn't it figure they had availability last minute for her shower? But her mother was right. She was getting the wedding she wanted. Small. Simple. And at the house so, God forbid, it would be easy to cancel if she needed to.

The constant worry weighing on her about whether Thom would get home in time had become so much of a part of her life, she had gotten used to it. But he had assured her—as much as he could given nothing was certain—that he'd be back in time. She had to trust him.

Maybe she shouldn't have chosen the full moon right after he left. She should have picked one later in the year.

Second guessing herself didn't help. It was too

late now. The invitations had already gone out. She'd arranged for the tables and chairs. Ordered the flowers for her bouquet from the florist and the food from the gourmet shop.

Now all she needed was the groom.

A knock on the door had her abandoning the laundry basket of clean clothes as her mother continued to list menu items. Ginny moved to the door and peered through the peephole . . . and nearly dropped the cell phone at what she saw.

It took both hands to get the locks undone and the door opened but she managed it, flinging the door wide.

She jumped him, throwing her arms around Thom's neck and kissing him as all of the pent up worry flooded out of her.

When she finally moved back to let him in, he frowned, looking at her hand. "Are you on the phone?"

Ginny widened her eyes and smothered a curse. Pressing the forgotten cell in her hand to her ear she said, "Mom. Mom." It took Ginny twice to get her mother to hear her while she continued to talk. "Can I call you back?"

"Um, okay."

"Thom just got here." Ginny nearly bubbled over with the news.

"Oh, thank God."

For once, Ginny couldn't agree with her mother more. She blew out a breath as her heart pounded. "I know."

"Okay I'll let you go. And I'll call Molly and tell her."

"Yes, please. Thank you. Call you later." Ginny disconnected the call and went back to looking at the vision before her. "Oh, my God. I was so worried. Why didn't you call me or text?"

"I did. I texted the minute we hit the tarmac that I was home safe."

"What time?" she asked.

"Like about one."

"In the morning?"

"Yes, in the morning. See?" He lifted one brow high. "I know you hate military time but this is why it's easier. If I'd said zero-one-hundred versus thirteen-hundred you wouldn't have to ask to know if I meant morning or afternoon."

"Easier for you maybe." She didn't want to debate the merits of the twenty-four hour clock. They had too much lost time to make up for. "Anyway, I didn't get the text."

"I was wondering why you didn't reply. Sorry, baby. Sometimes reception is spotty at the airfield. I should have sent another."

"It's okay. I can't believe you're really back."

"I know. I keep feeling like I need to knock wood so I don't jinx it. In fact . . . " Thom reached out and knocked on the wooden table near the door.

Ginny did the same, suddenly superstitious when she never used to be.

"So, I've got two weeks leave and nothing to do. Got any suggestions?" His voice dropped low and sexy as he edged closer.

She smiled. "Maybe one."

He leaned in and kissed her, his facial hair tickling her lips.

Pulling back, she ran her hands over his beard, soft beneath her fingers. "I'm not used to so much of this."

When Thom wasn't clean shaven, he usually had a short cropped beard.

"I know. Sorry. We've been deploying so much I've let it grow in. It helps us blend with the locals. You should see some of the rest of the guys. Rocky's beard could probably win a contest at this point."

She lifted a brow. "Oh."

He laughed at her reaction. "I'll clean up in time for the wedding. Don't worry." Thom moved in for another kiss and then paused. "Unless you want me to shave now?"

As he held her close, with two large warm hands on her hips, she pressed against the very tantalizing outline of his need for her. That only increased her own ever growing desire to have him. Now. Naked, over her, in her bed.

"No. Leave it." She wasn't going to break this spell by letting him take the time to shave. They had days before the ceremony. He had time.

His mouth was temptingly close already. She reached up and pulled him closer, until another thought hit her.

"Oh, my God." Her eyes widened. "I just thought of something. How are the kids going to get here for the wedding? Are you driving back to Virginia and getting them?"

That would take him away from her again. She didn't like that idea.

Thom pulled back and pressed his lips together.

He drew in a breath and finally met her gaze. "No. Debbie isn't going to let them come."

"What? Why not?"

He shrugged. "Why does she do anything she does? Who knows?"

Ginny frowned. "Did you ask her?"

"Of course, I asked her. I got back late last night and stopped over there this morning before I left for here. I saw the kids. I knew she wasn't going to want them to be away for two weeks, but still, I was hoping she'd—" He shook his head. "Never mind. It just gets me pissed talking about it. Anyway, I was so upset I just got back in the car and drove straight here."

Ginny hated seeing him upset.

What if he'd been so upset he'd forgotten what he'd need for the wedding?

"Um, did you happen to remember to bring your dress uniform with you for the ceremony?"

His mouth crooked up with a small smile. "Yes, my little worrier. I had my SUV packed with everything I'd need before I even left the country. Just in case we got back late and I had to rush to make it up here."

"So organized," she teased. "Like a boy scout."

He drew his brows low. "No. Like a SEAL. Now come here and welcome me back properly."

"Gladly." She moved closer even as her mind spun with ideas. She was going to find a way to get those kids there for the wedding—for Thom—if it was the last thing she did.

CHAPTER SIXTEEN

"You sure you're okay with me being away so close to the wedding?" Thom asked.

"Little late to ask now, bro," Brody said from the passenger seat.

Thom shushed him as Ginny answered, "Of course. I'm fine. Don't worry. Having you in the next state is a nice change from the usual."

"Not exactly the next state but yeah, it is a nice change. So we'll be back tomorrow night. Okay?" They'd have to be back because the following morning was his wedding day. Thom tried not to panic about that.

"Yup. That's fine."

"I'll stop by to see you when we get back and grab my uniform from your place but I'm going to sleep at my parents' house tomorrow night since I shouldn't see you before the ceremony." It was kind of an outdated tradition, but he didn't need to tempt any bad luck.

"Okay. But remember, I arranged for the photographer to be at the church at nine to take pictures. He'll photograph us separately before the ceremony, then together after—" Ginny's voice cut out and then faded completely.

Thom pulled the cell away from his ear and looked at the display. "Shit. No bars."

"Yeah. I'm not surprised. We never had good signal driving here. Sorry." At the wheel, Rocky met Thom's gaze in the rearview mirror.

Thom sighed. "Not your fault." He tossed the phone on the seat next to him and looked at the passing scenery, getting more wooded with every mile they traveled. "We almost there?"

Brody laughed. "Who needs kids when we have Thom in the backseat asking *are we there yet?*"

"Mm, hm," Rocky agreed. "And the answer is yes, we're almost there."

That was a bit of an exaggeration since it was a solid hour before Rocky slowed and steered his pickup truck off the main road and onto a dirt one.

As they bounced along, hitting enough puddles and potholes to make Thom have to grab the front seats to hold on, he understood why Rocky had said they'd need his truck with the four-wheel drive.

"And where are we again?" Brody asked.

"The Poconos, southern boy."

"Pennsylvania," Thom clarified, figuring Alabama-born Brody wouldn't know where the Poconos were either.

"And you're from here?" Brody asked, glancing around at the deserted solitude around them.

"No. My family's in Trenton."

At Brody's blank stare in response to Rocky's answer, Thom clarified, "That's in New Jersey."

"Oh."

Rocky shook his head at Brody. "Dude. I'm gonna buy you a map."

"I have a map if I need one. On my phone."

"Which doesn't work up here," Thom reminded.

"Looks like lover boy is having withdrawal already because he can't talk to the future wife." Brody laughed, glancing over his shoulder at Thom.

"Well, in my defense, if I'd known there was no signal up here I would have told her in advance."

"Whipped already," Rocky added and then said, "And we're here."

After another giant hole that listed the truck to one side, Rocky slowed to pull between two fence posts.

Thom leaned between the seats. "Where's the cabin?"

When Brody and Thom exchanged glances, Rocky shook his head. "It's another half a mile up the right-of-way. Don't worry. It exists. I promise. We won't be sleeping outside."

"Wouldn't be the first time." Brody snorted.

"Nope," Thom agreed.

True to his word, Rocky steered the truck up to a log cabin that actually didn't look too bad. The stovepipe coming out of the roof proved there was heat for the colder months. The front porch, complete with wooden Adirondack chairs, was just waiting for them to crack a beer and kick back.

After throwing the truck into park and cutting the

engine, Rocky pulled out the keys and twisted in his seat. "Somebody grab the cooler. I'll unlock the door and see about firing up the charcoal grill."

Barbecued meat and beer. Thom couldn't argue with Rocky's priorities. "I'll get it."

A few minutes later Thom was taking advantage of that porch—and the chairs and the beer as the coals got hot enough to grill their steaks.

Stretching his legs out, he took a sip of cold brew and sighed.

There might be no electric or running water, but there was a helluva shooting range set up behind the cabin. He intended to take advantage of that shortly.

As far as bachelor parties went, Thom couldn't have asked for anything better.

Sure, it was just the three of them, but he was fine with that. Low key. Less chance of them getting into trouble than if everyone were here. Things could get crazy when they were in a group.

Besides, expecting all of the guys in the platoon to request leave to come to New England early for his bachelor party as well as the wedding would have been asking too much. As it was he wasn't sure if anyone else from the team would be able to make it to the wedding.

He had left Virginia close to a week ago and hadn't talked to most of the guys since. Theirs would probably be one of the last minute RSVPs Ginny had said she was still getting in the mail.

Thom had given all the guys the address of the cabin and the dates of when he'd be there, along with an open invite. They knew they were welcome to come for any part of the time if they could make it, no advance notice necessary. So there was a chance this little party could get much larger. But if they couldn't make it, that would be fine too. Having Brody and Rocky with him for a relaxing couple of days suited Thom just fine.

Rocky stood on the front porch of the cabin and gazed out over the woods surrounding them. "Twenty-four hours of nothing but peace and quiet."

"And of shooting at shit with the guys." Thom added.

"Yup. That too." Rocky grinned.

Brody frowned at them both. "You do realize that pretty much describes our job. Right?"

"Yeah, but here nobody's shooting back at us." Thom laughed.

"And there are no instructors rating our performance," Rocky added before he raised a beer bottle to his lips.

Thom headed for the cooler to grab himself another beer since his seemed to be almost empty, when he paused. "We doing any shooting today?"

"Eh, we got all day tomorrow. How about we make today all about eating and—more importantly—drinking and we play with the guns tomorrow?"

"When we might be too hung over to drink anymore anyway so we'll be good and sober for target practice, you mean?" Brody asked.

"Yup." Rocky nodded.

Brody laughed. "That sounds good, cause I'm fixin' to be too drunk to handle a weapon tonight anyway."

Thom smiled and reached his hand into the ice of the cooler. He thought he was pulling out a bottle of beer but emerged instead with a bottle of bourbon.

Thom cocked a brow at Rocky, who'd packed the cooler, as he held up the bottle of liquor. "You put any soda in here with this?"

"Ah, shit. That's what I forgot." Rocky's grin didn't make him look like he'd really forgotten.

Shaking his head, Thom reached back in for a beer. This was going to be one hell of a night.

CHAPTER SEVENTEEN

The hangover was fierce. Sharp and blinding above the neck and almost worse below where Thom's stomach was doing flips that seemed to reach up into his throat.

He stumbled out to the front porch after making a trip out back to the outhouse. Thom found Brody already outside, gathering wood to start a fire.

"What are you doing?" Thom squinted against the glare of the morning sun.

"I'm fixin' to start breakfast but we only brought one bag of charcoal." Brody straightened from where he'd been bent over piling the sticks in the stone fire pit and looked toward Thom. "I think the better question is how are you doing?"

"I've been better." He pressed a hand to his head, which only made Brody smile wider. As his brain started to function, he noticed a few key absences. "Where's Rocky? And the truck?"

"City boy ran out for coffee. Didn't believe I could brew it on the fire."

"How far is he gonna have to go to find coffee around here?"

"Couldn't be too far. I hear the truck now." Brody cocked his head to the side.

How the fuck was Brody functioning and not hung over? Thom decided to figure that out later. After coffee.

He made his way gingerly down the few short steps to the ground as Rocky pulled up close to the cabin and cut the engine.

When he swung the door open and stepped down, Thom nearly wept with joy at the cardboard holder in his hand bearing three extra-large to-go cups.

Rocky strode forward, one cup held out in offering. "Good morning, sunshine. Coffee?"

"Oh, bless you. Yes."

"Hung over?" Rocky laughed.

"Yes. Why aren't you?" Thom frowned.

Rocky shrugged. "Maybe I can handle my alcohol better than you."

Or maybe his two supposed friends had plied him with extra liquor. Even if they had, Thom couldn't be angry as the hot coffee slid down his throat.

"There's ibuprofen in my bag." Rocky eyed him again. "You know, in case you need it."

Hell yeah, he needed it. "Thanks." Thom was about to go in search of relief when he heard the loud *crack* cut through the woods.

Rocky glanced in the direction of the unmistakable sound. "Somebody's up and out shooting early."

That single shot was followed by a burst of a dozen rounds of rapid fire.

"What the fuck? That's no hunting rifle." Thom eyed the woods.

"Who the hell is shooting a semi-automatic weapon up here?" Brody asked.

The sound began again, with more than one weapon being fired this time.

Thom frowned. "How close is the nearest neighbor?"

Rocky shook his head. "I don't know. Last time I was here, there was an old farmer who owned all the acreage on either side of us. But I haven't been here in a long time. He could've sold."

Brody let out a snort. "I don't know about around here but I don't know any farmers who make a habit of shooting up their places with an AR-15."

"Me either," Thom said. "We need to check this out."

"Hell, yeah, we do." Brody planted his coffee down on the rail and spun toward the staircase.

"We're on leave. We don't have to do shit if we don't want to, you know." Rocky looked from Brody to Thom and then let out a sigh, putting his own cup down. "There goes my peace and quiet."

"Do we go armed?" Thom asked.

It wasn't like they were set up for a recon mission. They'd come prepared with beer and food for the barbecue, not body armor or weapons or anything else they'd normally have when heading out.

"Hell yeah, we go armed." Brody turned to Rocky. "What've we got here?"

"Um, my grandfather's double barrel shotgun. A couple of twenty-twos. Buckshot. Birdshot. And some knives."

"So we're roughing it." Thom cocked a brow.

"Hey. What do you want from me?" Rocky frowned. "It's not even hunting season. We came here to relax and shoot at targets. Not get in a firefight with the neighbors."

"We're not going to get in a firefight with anybody," Thom said, worried by the gleam he saw in Brody's eyes.

Brody let out a snort. "Not with our choice of weapons against what they've got, we're not. Talk about bringing a knife to a gun fight."

"We're just gonna check on what's going on. Maybe it's just a couple of guys enjoying some time away, just like us." Why did Thom feel like he had to supervise Brody? It wasn't even his cabin. He turned to Rocky, looking for help.

Rocky pressed his lips together. "All right. We check it out."

"Armed?" Brody asked.

"Yes, armed." Rocky rolled his eyes. "Good thing my grandfather isn't around to see this."

Brody was already inside checking out the gun cabinet Rocky had unlocked when they'd arrived. He held up the double barrel. "You're nuts. The man who owns this quality weapon would most definitely approve of what we're doing."

Rocky glanced at Thom and tipped his head toward Brody. "Guess he's taking the double barrel."

"Guess so." Thom laughed.

Thom grabbed one of the .22s, squinting at the name on it. "A Henry. Nice."

Brody's head whipped up. "That's a Henry rifle?"

Thom pulled the gun close to his chest and frowned at Brody. "Oh, no. You picked your gun already. This one is mine."

Another round of shooting began in the distance and sobered Thom immediately. "We need to get out there."

"Agreed." Rocky pulled open drawers and started tossing ammo and knives onto the table.

They grabbed their weapons, shoved extra ammo in the cargo pockets of their pants, along with the knives and headed out the door.

As the three of them went outside Thom figured they would check out the source of the noise and then, when they found it was nothing but a couple of guys having fun, they could come back and continue their guys' getaway.

If nothing else, they'd have an interesting story to tell at the wedding.

They moved through the woods like the well-trained commandos they were. Their training was so ingrained in them, into their minds, their muscles and reflexes, it didn't matter if they were sneaking into an insurgent stronghold or a hunting camp the procedure was the same.

This could have been any one of the exercises they routinely ran through between missions to keep their skills sharp. Any live-ammo tactical scenario staged in a wooded terrain.

Except it wasn't a training exercise . . .

It could, however, turn out to be an exercise in futility if all they found were a bunch of drunk guys taking their target practice to the extreme by shooting off a couple of hundred rounds from their AR-15s.

Whoever the shooters were, they were still at it. It was sporadic, but the sound of gunfire hadn't stopped for more than a few minutes since when the three of them had left the cabin in pursuit of answers.

The bursts of sound increased in volume as they progressed through the woods. Thom, Brody and Rocky were definitely getting closer. Close enough they slowed their pace and began to move more quietly as they approached.

Maybe they were being overly cautious, but they didn't know what they were walking into. Then again, maybe they were being foolish not being *more* cautious because they didn't know what they were walking into.

Armed with hunting guns and not much more, this might be the stupidest thing they could have done. Normal people probably would have gone to the police to report the gunfire. SEALs tended to handle things on their own.

When Thom began to hear voices he knew they were almost upon the group of shooters. He gave Brody and Rocky the signal to hold where they were.

"There looks like there's a clearing just ahead." Thom tipped his chin toward where it looked as if the forest got less dense.

"I smell smoke. And . . ." Brody sniffed the air. "Barbecue."

"I told you. It's probably just a group of guys hanging—" Rocky didn't finish the sentence as his eyes widened and he stared at something past Thom's shoulder.

"What?" Thom swiveled his head to look just as the foliage behind him moved. The same happened three more places as the woods around them came to life.

"Ghillie suits," Brody hissed.

Thom nodded.

The question was why in the mountains of Pennsylvania were there men hiding in the woods, camouflaged as well as any military commando and outfitted with automatic weapons, which happened to be pointed directly at them?

"Put them guns down." The order came from one of the invisible men who'd become visible when he stepped out from a bush behind Rocky holding what looked like it could be an AR-15 draped in camo netting.

"A'ight." Brody nodded, bending slowly to lay the double barrel on the ground. Thom and Rocky did the same with their rifles.

As Thom clasped his hands behind his head so none of these guys would mistake any move he made as him going for a handgun and then shoot him, he took inventory of what else he had on him that could be used as a weapon.

The folding knife he'd shoved in his pocket, his training and his wits were the sum total of what he had to defend himself with.

They were outmanned and outgunned. And the four surrounding them were just the men they could see. There were more men at the camp, as evidenced by the voices Thom still heard.

He supposed he'd be seeing them soon. One man clicked on a comm unit not quite as high tech as what they used in the teams but military grade.

"Intruders in the perimeter. Requesting back up."

"Who the fuck are these—"

"Shut up!" One man cut off Rocky's question and silenced any further discussion among them.

Whoever they were dealing with, it was best to humor them for now.

Once Thom and the guys figured out the situation and what they were up against, they could decide how to get themselves out of it. Because just like their current captors were an unknown entity, so too were Brody, Rocky and Thom to them.

There was no way these men, whoever they were, suspected they had three of Uncle Sam's most highly trained operators in their possession. And Thom intended to keep it that way.

The fact they came armed with nothing but Rocky's granddad's rifles and were staying at his family's cabin helped the ruse that they were just three normal untrained civilian guys hanging out.

Confident they'd be able to bullshit their way out of this situation Thom maintained his calm . . . until a dozen more men showed up, these kitted out as well if not better than their ghillie-suited friends, right down to the Kevlar vests and KA-BAR knives.

"Shit," Rocky said on a breath.

Thom couldn't agree more. This might not be as easy to get out of as he'd anticipated, even for them.

CHAPTER EIGHTEEN

"Have you heard from Thom today?" Ginny asked her soon-to-be mother-in-law.

"Not today, no. Actually, not since he left for his boys' trip. Is everything all right?"

"I guess so. It's just that when he called me on the way to the cabin yesterday we got cut off and he never called back."

"Oh, I'm sure that's nothing to worry about. You said he's somewhere near the Poconos?" Thom's mother asked.

"Yes."

"We have friends who go skiing in that area every year and they say there's terrible cell service." The older woman leaned forward. "I bet that's why these men like their hunting cabins in the mountains so much. They have a good excuse to not answer their phones when their wives call."

Ginny liked the idea that she'd be one of those wives in less than twenty-four hours once she and Thom officially said *I do*.

She smiled. "You're right. The connection was terrible while he was able to talk to me. He did say they would be home tonight, though I'm not sure what time."

He'd better not be too late or he'd be tired for the wedding in the morning.

Directly on the heels of that thought Ginny remembered Thom telling her how little sleep he and the team usually got and how they'd work what he called vampire hours. She supposed she couldn't expect him to be tucked in bed at nine p.m. like she'd be tonight so she wouldn't look tired in the wedding pictures.

"If they're having a good time, I imagine they'll stay as late as they can. Boys will be boys and he and his friends on the team get so little time off, they'll want to take advantage of every minute."

"Probably," Ginny agreed.

It was hard to be worried around Thom's mother. The woman was perpetually like a ray of sunshine. She brightened everything she touched.

"You do realize if it rains the reception will be ruined because we didn't rent a tent." Ginny's mother, on the other hand, was the polar opposite of Thom's mom. Today, she'd chosen to be the voice of gloom and doom regarding the weather as she swept into the dining room from the adjoining kitchen.

"Our next door neighbor owns a couple of those

little blue pop-up canopy things," Thom's mother offered. "I'll call and ask if we can borrow them, just in case of rain. We probably should anyway. We can set them up to keep the sun off the food and drink tables. The weather channel said it's going to be a beautiful day."

Ginny's mom let out a huff as she sat. "When has the weather man ever been right?"

Molly, seated between the two mothers at the dining room table, said, "Rain or shine, I'm sure the tents will come in handy. We should definitely try to borrow them."

It was like watching a ping pong match. The pessimist versus the optimist and Molly was the referee. Ginny would be amused if it weren't her wedding day they were talking about.

She glanced down at the table, spread with lists and response cards from the guests, which were still trickling in even with the wedding day so close. That was to be expected she supposed since, out of necessity, she'd sent the invitations out a bit later than popular convention dictated she should.

Her mother sat and reached for one of the lists. Beneath it Ginny spied an unopened envelope. She reached for it and tore it open, sighing when she didn't recognize the name.

"Who's that from?" her mother asked.

"Jack and Evelyn." Ginny squinted at the scribble on the card. "Some last name I can't read."

"Jack and Evelyn Jacobson. They're on our side," Thom's mother supplied. "Old friends of the family. I hope it's okay I invited them. You'd given me those invitations to mail out to our list."

She had misinterpreted Ginny's disappointment. It had nothing to do with who Thom's family had invited and everything to do with who Ginny herself had mailed one last minute invitation to.

Ginny waved aside her concern. "No. Of course. It's fine. You can invite whoever you want."

There was one reply she was waiting for specifically, but so far it hadn't arrived.

She drew in a breath and decided the best way to take her mind off everything weighing on it was to keep busy. "So, who's ready to tie some birdseed sachets?"

CHAPTER NINETEEN

"I'm gonna ask you again. Who. Are. You!" The round-faced man, unidentifiable under the amount of camo grease paint he'd smeared on himself, asked the question with such fervor he spit at Rocky in the process.

Since all three of them had their hands bound behind their backs with plastic zip ties, which their captors had strangely had on hand in bulk, there wasn't much Rocky could do to defend himself from the flying splatter of spittle. He pulled his head back and narrowed his eyes against the saliva attack.

With his nose still wrinkled in distaste, Rocky answered for the second time. "I told you. My last name is Mangiano. My family owns the cabin not even a mile from here. If you'd check it out, you'll see. My pickup truck's parked there now. Go look at the name on the registration. Or better yet, call my father in New Jersey. Or my uncle. They'll—"

"Shut up!"

Rocky frowned. "Which do you want me to do? Answer your questions or shut up?"

Thom pressed his lips together, wondering if Rocky's tactic to antagonize the men holding them at gunpoint while their hands were bound was a wise one.

He shot Brody a glance. Brody's gaze shifted sideways to meet Thom's as he lifted an eyebrow.

They'd already been frisked and their meager stash of weapons as well as their cell phones taken from them.

Now they sat on three wooden chairs around a small square table inside a plywood building that smelled of cigarette smoke and body odor intermingled with burnt bacon.

It was a pretty nauseating combination. But no more nauseating than the fact they'd let themselves stumble right into the hands of these military wannabes.

And that's what they had to be—men playing war because it was becoming apparent these guys weren't active military or even veterans. They seemed more like a group of guys who'd assembled themselves to form some sort of self-appointed citizens militia.

What Thom hadn't decided yet was if they were dangerous. Were they armed to the teeth in some misguided effort to defend the United States, or did they have a different, more damaging and far more dangerous agenda in mind?

Terrorists didn't have to look or sound like Abu Bakr al-Baghdadi. Thom knew they could just as easily be a blonde haired, blue-eyed guy who goes by the name of Bubba, or possibly Junior.

Meanwhile, while they worked on figuring a way out of this mess, Thom really wished Rocky would pocket his New Jersey attitude and play nice with the homegrown terrorists.

"You!" The apparent leader of this motley crew had obviously had enough of Rocky and his smart ass attitude.

He moved to stand in front of Brody, who was staring down at the floor refusing to make eye contact with him.

The man kicked Brody's boot. Only then did Brody raise his eyes and answer, in his slowest southern drawl, "Uh, yeah?"

"What are you doing here?"

Brody frowned. "You brought me here."

The man narrowed his eyes. "I meant what were you doing here in the woods?"

"Well, I was hoping to get drunk and shoot up some shit."

Thom couldn't hide the twitch of his lips at the response from Brody, cool as his southern grandmother's cucumber sandwiches in spite of this volatile situation. What struck Thom as the funniest part was that Brody was telling the absolute truth.

"What the fuck are you smiling at?" The man leaned in close to Thom as he spoke, thereby blowing a cloud of breath so bad it should have been visible directly into his face.

"I wasn't aware I was smiling."

"How about *you* try telling me what you're doing here?"

"Exactly like he said. We came to drink and shoot. Just like you guys." Thom tipped his head toward the two guards in the room with them. "Just like you, we're up here to shoot some guns so why don't you just let us go?"

It was a shot in the dark, but hell, it was worth a try.

One of the guards let out a *pfft*. "With those guns you had on you? Fuck no, you're not just like us. This is a gun." He shook his weapon at Thom. "Those things you had are just . . . antiques."

The other guy chortled in agreement. "Yeah, they belong in a museum."

One scathing glare from their not-so-esteemed leader silenced the two guards before he turned back to Thom. "If that's true, then why the fuck are you here in my camp making me look at your ugly faces?"

Thom flashed back to BUD/S when the instructors used to yell insults at the training class while trying to get them to ring out. It hadn't worked then and it wasn't going to work now.

Hell, here he was warm and dry and was operating on a full night's sleep. That right there were just three things he hadn't had benefit of during Hell Week and he hadn't quit then. All three of them seated here had made it through then. They'd make it through now.

Meanwhile they were still awaiting Thom's answer in this circular line of questioning that never went anywhere. "Because you're keeping us here?"

The oversized man narrowed his eyes and Thom braced himself. He wouldn't put it past these guys to take a swing at him even if his hands were tied.

Of course that didn't mean he couldn't defend himself. The idiots had left their feet unbound and hadn't even tied them to the chair.

They *had* bound their hands behind their back rather than in front but that just made the confines more uncomfortable not more secure.

The three of them had been through the Navy's SERE training—more than once. Okay, so today they'd obviously failed at the *evasion* part of the Survival, Evasion, Resistance and Escape class, but they'd make up for it in the *escape* portion.

Thom knew Brody and Rocky would be taking in the details, observing their surroundings and weighing the options, just waiting for an opportunity, just like he was.

They were a team. Training together. Fighting together. He didn't need words to know what they were thinking.

"Do you really expect me to believe you three," the man scowled as he waggled his finger back and forth between them, "are just shooting buddies?"

Thom tipped his head in a nod. "Yes."

"Then tell me this, how come he sounds like a redneck, he sounds like a mobster and you sound like you went to Harvard?" He tipped his head to Brody and Rocky in turn before zeroing in on Thom.

As dumb as he looked, he'd still picked up on the fact the three of them were from three different states in three distinct parts of the country—the deep south, New England and New Jersey.

The military brought together and made lifelong friends out of people from all over the country, but Thom sure as hell wasn't going to tell Bubba here that.

Their training was their ace in the hole. Thom didn't want their captors to know he and the guys had the skills to break out of there if these men were dumb enough to leave them unguarded for even a moment.

Besides that, telling yahoos like these guys he was military would just be asking for trouble. They'd no doubt feel they had something to prove. Would want to show off by beating the big bad Navy SEALs.

Nope. Thom wasn't about to tell the truth this time, but he figured he didn't have to because there was another place that brought together people from disparate backgrounds and locations and it would be just as believable as the truth.

"We all went to college together." He kept the lie short and sweet. No need to elaborate where or when if they didn't ask and most likely, they wouldn't ask.

The man's face contorted, making it even uglier than usual as he sneered. "College boys. That figures. Always sticking their noses where they don't belong—"

A man entered the cabin. "Ray."

Thom made a mental note of the man's name as his buddy interrupted him.

"What!"

"We sent a recon team out to check on the perimeter." The new arrival tried his best to give an official sounding report.

"And?" Ray asked.

"Nothing. They didn't see anything."

"Then why the hell are you bothering me?"

"Um, because you said you wanted a report."

The two formerly silent guards chuckled. They'd been manning the corners of the approximate ten by twelve foot room with weapons more suited for long range shooting, not close quarter combat.

In this tight space, those long barrels were going to do nothing but get in the way and stop them from being able to take a shot, and that's exactly what Thom was going to use to his advantage if given the opportunity.

Ray, obviously thinking he was the leader of this weird cult of men playing war, shook his head. He turned his back on the new man, who took a solid minute before he figured out he had been dismissed. As Ray ignored him, he stood there and shuffled from one foot to the other until he finally took the hint and left.

Thom was waiting for Ray's next move, so he could decide his, when the sound of the crack of a rifle shot brought all of their heads up.

"Who the fuck is that shooting? I suspended all range practice until we straighten this shit out." Ray spun to stride toward the door.

Thom didn't know, but since the shot had drawn Ray and the two guards all outside at once, he had to think he liked the new odds of them getting out of there sooner rather than later.

"What the fuck are you two idiots doing out here? Get back in there and watch them!"

Or, maybe not . . .

Thom heard Brody sigh and Rocky let out a low curse, and silently agreed with both of them.

CHAPTER TWENTY

Clad in a robe over her pajamas, Molly checked her cell phone. "Twelve hours from now you're supposed to be saying your vows."

"I know." Ginny didn't miss the words *supposed to be* in Molly's announcement.

She'd thought having Molly spend the night at her place the night before the wedding would keep her calm.

It hadn't worked out that way. This adult sleepover for her and her maid of honor had done nothing but stress Ginny out.

Molly obsessively monitored the time and announced it as regularly as Big Ben. Ginny was ready to steal Molly's phone and hide it so she'd at least have to go to the kitchen to look at the time on the microwave if she wanted to announce it.

Ginny stifled a sigh. Molly meant well. She knew that. But Ginny didn't have the strength to deal with both the complete lack of communication from Thom since he'd left *and* her maid of honor repeatedly reminding her about how close the wedding was while her groom was still missing.

She should have spent tonight alone. All she wanted to do was go to bed—not that she'd be able to sleep. Not until she knew Thom was safely back from the cabin and at his parents' house.

Molly drew in a breath. "And remember we're going to have to get to the church early to take pictures. That's in exactly eleven hours."

"I know," Ginny repeated.

Pictures. She was going to look like crap in the photos, with big dark circles under her eyes that even every product on the shelves in Sephora wouldn't be able to camouflage.

It figured that the one tradition Ginny hadn't fought her mother on, the one she'd given in to whole heartedly, was hiring a professional photographer for their special day.

Now she only hoped there'd be a groom to stand next to her in the photos.

Molly continued to watch Ginny too intensely for her to be able to relax. "Aren't you worried you haven't heard from him? That he's not back yet?" Molly asked.

"No. I'm sure they just lost track of time." Ginny waved away her friends concern, delivering the lie with as much conviction as she could muster.

The truth was she had passed worry quite a while ago. It had hit her right after mild concern and just before the heart pounding panic she was experiencing now. The tight knot formed again in her belly and this time spread, moving up into her chest.

She tried to talk herself down from the ledge one more time, like she'd been doing for most of the evening. If they'd left after dinner at seven or even eight they wouldn't get home until after ten or eleven. But by now they should have good enough cell phone signal to call her . . . *if* their phones weren't all dead.

Of course! That had to be it. They were men. Men never remembered details like packing a charger. And it would have to be a car charger too since Thom had joked before he left how they'd be roughing it because the cabin had no electricity.

So they could easily be on the way back right now and just not able to call or text because all of their batteries were dead.

Maybe he was already back at his parents' house and hadn't texted or called because it was so late and he didn't want to wake her on the night before the wedding.

She felt moderately better with her new excuse for the lack of communications. Good enough to take a sip of the herbal tea Molly had made for her—her friend's attempt at calming her, when just not bringing up the subject that had upset her in the first place would have worked much better than the Sleepy Time Tea.

Ginny glanced up to find Molly watching her with that look again. The look that said her best friend thought she was being delusional.

Molly would see. In the morning, when Thom showed up at the church right on time and explained how he'd forgotten his charger, Ginny's faith in him would be proven justified.

He would apologize. She would forgive him. They'd get married and then they'd pose for pictures together, and she didn't intend to look like death warmed over because she hadn't slept.

She quickly did the math. She could take a sleeping pill right now and still get eight hours sleep even if she woke up early to get ready. Perfect.

"Siri. Set an alarm for six-thirty in the morning," Ginny said into her cell phone as she walked toward the bathroom.

"Alarm set for six-thirty a.m.," the feminine computerized voice replied.

"Thank you." Even though Siri was an AI assistant, it felt rude to not express any gratitude.

She came out of the bathroom with a bottle of over-the-counter sleeping pills and headed toward where she'd left her tea on the table.

Molly frowned. "What are you doing?"

"Taking something so I can go to sleep."

"But what if you're groggy in the morning or what if you don't wake up in time?"

"That's what you and Siri are here for, to make sure I wake up. And if I don't take something I won't get to sleep and then I'll *definitely* be groggy tomorrow so I'm willing to take my chances."

Herbal tea wasn't going to cut it tonight. Not with all the stress surrounding this wedding.

Enough listening to everyone else about what was best for her. Ginny knew what she needed, and short of having Thom in bed next to her tonight, the sleeping pill and a solid eight hours would be the next best thing.

Before Molly tried to talk her out of it, she popped the pill into her mouth and swallowed it with a big gulp of minty lukewarm tea.

Done. Nothing to do now except try to have sweet dreams and then wake up and get married.

Easy. No problem at all . . .

CHAPTER TWENTY-ONE

Time ticked by, as evidenced by the shadows moving down the wall and across the floor through the one dirty window as the sun set. The room grew darker as the light diminished—just like Thom's optimism.

The guards changed twice over the hours as one pair of men left and another pair took their places, which only meant these guys were fresh and less likely to screw up.

Ray came in twice more, asking the same questions, not believing the same answers—the only answers Thom and the guys were willing to give.

Their hands had been unbound and they were given a bucket to piss in once during the long day— at gunpoint in a room full of guards because apparently Ray had decided the three of them even unarmed were a threat. Since they'd been given no water to drink, once had been enough.

Thom smelled food being cooked outdoors but they weren't offered any. Ray must think they'd be more likely to spill their secrets if they were hungry. Thom would rather not eat anything prepared by their captors anyway.

The only real surprise was that there was none of the drinking or revelry that Thom had expected from this group as night fell. Instead, the camp went dead quiet shortly after full dark. Though it wasn't all that dark because, as he'd requested, Ginny had planned their wedding for the full moon.

Thoughts of Ginny and their wedding, now mere hours away, fueled Thom's drive to get out of there.

They didn't talk. Brody and Rocky stayed silent, just like Thom. At one point Brody looked as if he was asleep. Knowing Brody—who could sleep anytime and anywhere—he might actually be taking a short nap, although just as likely was that he was pretending, a ruse to lull the guards into a false sense of security.

It was a good idea. Thom dropped his chin to his chest and closed his eyes but his ears remained open. He listened closely to the guards' breathing, to the sound of them shifting in the chairs they'd finally settled in after growing tired of standing during their shift, to the shuffling of their boots against the floor.

It had to be close to an hour that he waited but eventually Thom heard the change. The slow steady deep breaths of one guard. The soft snore from another.

Two guards and by all indications both asleep.

Head still down, he opened his eyes a crack. The men watching them were slumped in their chairs, their guns laid across their knees.

He glanced toward Brody and Rocky and saw both of them raise their heads. Thom saw Brody's shoulders moving, rotating as the rest of him barely moved in the chair until finally he brought his hands around front.

Brody always had been like Houdini when it came to getting out of zip ties, even handcuffs, during trainings. It's like the man's joints popped in and out effortlessly. Thom didn't question it, just happy that now that Brody was free, he'd cut them all loose and Thom wouldn't have to dislocate his own thumb.

Reaching into his boot, Brody emerged with a small knife that Ray's men hadn't discovered during the shoddy search they'd conducted. He moved noiselessly to behind Rocky, cut his ties and then came to Thom and did the same.

Ignoring the stiffness in his joints from being bound and immobile for so many hours, Thom stood and looked to Brody. During an op they'd have rules of engagement, standard operating procedure. He'd know if he was supposed to disable the guards temporarily, or permanently, or bring them with him for questioning.

It was risky to try to sneak out of the room without waking the guards. The sound of the door opening could wake them and they didn't know what they'd encounter outside. Ray could very well have men set up on watch outside the door, as well as at the perimeter of the camp.

It would be best if Thom, Brody and Rocky were at least armed.

Rocky had already grabbed the double barrel shotgun the men had taken from them but had been dumb enough to leave in the room with them.

Brody signaled for Thom to take the man on the left and he would take the guard at the right.

They couldn't kill these men—they weren't at war even though it sure as hell felt like it—but they could choke them out, gag them and secure their hands with their own zip ties easily enough.

While Rocky held one gun at the ready, Thom and Brody moved into position.

With one swift simultaneous move, they had the guards in a headlock. With one hand over each man's mouth and the crook of their arms pressing on their throats, they compressed the carotid arteries with their biceps and forearms. Ten seconds later, both were unconscious.

Rocky ran forward and in quick work they had the two limp men gagged and bound, including their feet, before they regained consciousness.

Brody grabbed one of the automatic weapons, including extra clips, and Thom the other.

"Let's get the hell out of here." Rocky— obviously being foolishly sentimental, stood there loaded down with all three of his grandfather's weapons.

"Fine with me." Thom couldn't get out of there fast enough.

They moved to the door cautiously. They had an extremely limited window of opportunity before the two guards regained consciousness and started to make noise, or someone from outside came to check on them.

The camp had gone quiet hours ago. Thom hoped that meant everyone was sound asleep, hopefully inside the other buildings on the property where they couldn't see or hear the three men about to sneak away.

Brody eased the door open as Thom and Rocky flanked him on either side of the doorway. They might as well have been on an op. The process was the same and a successful outcome just as critical.

They needed to get far away and fast, hop in the truck and put some miles between them and this band of crazy gun-toting idiots. Only then would he be able to deal with the fallout of his being hours late getting back.

Brody led the way with Thom covering the rear since they were the two who had the firepower. Rocky was between them carrying the *museum relics*, as the guards had called them.

It was nearly impossible to move through densely wooded areas completely soundlessly. There was always the rustle of brush, the snap of twigs, the crunch of footsteps on the dry forest floor. Hopefully any guards stationed in the woods would assume it was an animal or their own men, possibly their relief, making the noise.

Thom had to believe that since—remembering the ghillie suits—there was no way he'd spot the camouflaged guards in the dark.

They were maybe a hundred yards out when Brody stopped dead. Rocky and Thom held fast and that's when Thom smelled what Brody must have, what had stopped him in his tracks. Cigarette smoke.

After a few seconds during which they all remained silent but heard no noise from the woods, Brody signaled for them to move to the left away from the scent, which seemed to have traveled to them on the breeze from the other direction.

The proof of someone in the woods with them, awake and smoking, meant their forward progress slowed to a crawl as remaining silent became even more crucial.

Slow and steady they progressed at an unnerving snail's pace, while with every step Thom braced himself for the sounds of the camp waking and discovering their absence.

They had bought themselves some time by tying the two gagged guards together with the length of rope that had been hanging on the wall. And then going the extra step of tying them to the legs of the cast iron wood stove in the room. Tight so they couldn't do much thrashing around and make enough noise for anyone nearby to hear.

Even so it was only a matter of time before the changing of the guard. Thom had intended on being long gone by that time. Hopefully on the highway headed East for Connecticut.

The pale gray on the horizon told Thom it was later than he'd thought. He was starting to fear the light was going to work against them just as they came upon a POSTED sign on a tree.

At the sight of the bright yellow sign Rocky took off at a run, moving past Brody to take the lead.

Far enough from the camp now to not worry as much about noise, Thom and Brody both followed until they broke into the clearing behind the cabin.

"Grab whatever you need and get in the truck." Rocky stomped up the stairs and flung the door wide. He emerged in seconds and tossed three duffle bags onto the porch before heading back inside. This time he emerged with the truck keys in his hand. He tossed his grandfather's guns inside the truck along with a metal ammo case, apparently not about to leave anything of value there for the men from the neighboring camp to find should they come looking.

Thom made a beeline for the cooler and dug into the melted ice for three bottles of water.

Food he could live without for a few more hours if he had to, but they were all dehydrated and needed water.

He'd started out the day thirsty from the night of drinking. After Ray's denying them anything to drink, Thom was even more so.

Brody scooped up the three duffels and the cooler and tossed it all in the bed of the truck, before jumping into the passenger seat.

Rocky let Thom into the back seat of the cab and then climbed behind the wheel. "Let's get the fuck out of here."

"The faster the better." Brody lowered the automatic window, the weapon he'd taken from the guard still at the ready, as if he expected a pursuit.

Hell, they might have a chase on their hands if Ray and his band of good old boys had discovered their captives gone and decided to jump in their trucks and come looking for them.

After shoving two bottles of water into the front cup holders for this teammates, Thom cracked open the third and took a gulp that half emptied it. He stowed the bottle in the back cup holder so he had two hands to hold the weapon he still carried.

"What are we gonna do about them back there?" Brody asked tipping his head back to indicate the whackos they were fleeing.

"We'll figure that out when we get far enough away. We can't go to the police. They'll have us in questioning for hours." Rocky glanced at Thom in the review mirror. "We have to get him back to Connecticut."

"Agreed. Besides, who knows where or how they got these weapons. I don't particularly like the idea of us waltzing into the police station with illegal firearms in our possession." Brody snorted out a short laugh. "I can't imagine command would be thrilled with that paper trail either."

"Or that three of their best-trained operators got taken by a bunch of yahoos in the woods of Pennsylvania," Rocky added.

"That too." Brody nodded. "Oh, shit. I'd forgotten we bought this."

Stowing the weapon, Brody reached beneath the dashboard and grabbed the packages of jerky they'd purchased at the gas station while Rocky had fueled up the truck during the drive there.

Brody ripped into the cellophane and distributed the contents to Rocky and Thom.

Thom tore off a bite. Even if his stomach was in knots, his body needed some fuel.

While chewing, Rocky said, "Okay, so how about this? As soon as we get back to civilization I'll call my father. He and my uncle have been coming up here since they were kids. Between them and my granddad, they've got contacts all over the area. They'll know who to call to take care of our *friends* back there without getting us into trouble." Rocky glanced at Thom again in the reflection of the mirror. "That good with you?"

"Yeah. It's good." Thom twisted in his seat. Sliding open the back window, he kept an eye on the roadway behind them.

The first order of business was to get the hell out of Dodge safely, then they could worry about all the rest.

CHAPTER TWENTY-TWO

Thom remained *good* for an hour or so, until the sun rose higher in the sky and he got a look at the clock on the dashboard. That's when he started to get antsy.

He was good at compartmentalizing things while in the middle of the action, but now that they were out of the shit, he was starting to lose it.

Another hour went by and he was crawling out of his skin, practically rocking with agitation and the adrenaline he couldn't expend in the backseat of a truck that wasn't getting him where he needed to go nearly fast enough.

The three-hour drive had felt like nothing on their way there two days ago.

Now, a day late getting back with no means of communication in their possession, the return trip felt like an eternity.

The time he should have been at the church, dressed and ready for photos, came and went and they were rapidly approaching the hour he was supposed to be standing with Ginny at the altar to take his vows.

Finally Thom cracked. "Oh. My. God. Why didn't we try and find our cell phones back there?"

Brody turned and cocked one brow. "Because we were escaping captivity by a bunch of lunatics?"

"And even if by some miracle we had gotten hold of a cell phone, I told you, the signal around here sucks," Rocky added.

Thom had managed to keep his cool during the captivity. To focus only on getting free as he'd been trained to do. To not obsess over Ginny and the wedding. But now that the imminent danger had passed, he was obsessing all right.

Good thing he'd long ago switched on the weapon's safety and put it down on the floorboards of the truck, because he was too twitchy to have his finger anywhere near the trigger of a loaded gun.

"But I called Ginny on the way here." Thom's frustration was starting to bubble over and spill onto his friends.

"And you talked for like thirty seconds before you lost the connection. This whole area is a dead zone. You were lucky to get a call to go through at all," said Rocky.

Thom saw nothing lucky about any part of his life over the past few days. In fact, he was most definitely the most unlucky man he knew.

His gut feeling had been right. Things had been going too smoothly—the successful raid in Iran, the delay-free transport back to the US, his two-week wedding leave being approved—so of course life had to slap him down and put him in his place.

If he was this crazy, then Ginny must be going completely insane.

Brody twisted in his seat to glance back at Thom. "Bro, we're gonna get there. A'ight?"

How could Brody be so confident? Thom frowned. "Do you not understand that the wedding is *today*?"

"Yup. *Later* today," Brody corrected.

Thom sniffed out a breath. "Not that much later."

They still had a long way to travel. And what if they hit traffic? Thom glanced at the digital display on the dashboard but all that did was upset him more.

"Dude. I'm driving as fast as I can."

Thom was well aware of that as he had to grab again for the back of the seats in front of him to keep from getting flung across the cab of the truck as Rocky veered from one lane to another, weaving in and out of traffic and passing the other vehicles that weren't going eighty-five miles an hour.

"Do you want me to get off the highway at the next exit and try to find a phone so you can call?" Rocky asked.

The likelihood of stumbling upon a pay phone nowadays was slim to none and it would take too long to find a gas station or convenience store and convince the clerk to let him use their landline to make a call.

"No. It's okay. We can't take the time. Just keep driving." He wouldn't feel better until he was in Stamford. He wouldn't be okay until they pulled into the parking lot of the church and he saw Ginny.

Rocky hit the brakes and Thom was flung against the seat in front of him.

"What the fuck?" Brody cursed.

"Cop," Rocky answered as he slowed to something more resembling the speed limit.

Fifteen minutes later, the police were the least of their problems as traffic slowed to a crawl.

"Can you see up ahead? What's going on?" Thom asked, tasting bile in the back of his throat.

"There's flashing lights. Must be an accident," Rocky answered. "We'll be past it in about half a mile."

Moving at five miles an hour the way they were, that'd only take—forever!

Shit. A camp full of gun-toting militants hadn't defeated Thom, but this drive just might.

CHAPTER TWENTY-THREE

"Virginia, I don't want to upset you, but is it possible he got cold feet?"

Shaking as her heart pounded, Ginny drew in a breath. "No, Mother. He didn't get cold feet."

"How can you be so sure?"

"I just can."

God, what if he got cold feet? The words swirled in her mind until her knees started to feel wobbly.

"I don't know how you're so certain—"

"Mother—" At the breaking point, and now full of doubt thanks to her mother, Ginny was about to lose it when her outburst was waylaid by Molly.

"Ginny, come with me to the bridal room so I can fix your hair." Molly didn't give Ginny a chance to respond as she dragged her off.

Molly pulled Ginny into the small room in the

back of the church the preacher had given them to use. Kind of part dressing room, part staging area.

She'd spent the morning in this room waiting for Thom to arrive, which he hadn't. She'd fixed her makeup in this mirror for the photos—which she'd faked a smile for. She wasn't sure she had anything left in her to fake anything else.

"What's wrong with my hair?" Ginny asked, knowing if one more thing went wrong she was going to end up in tears.

"Nothing, except I know you would have started to pull it out if I didn't get you away from that conversation."

"You're right." Ginny let out a sigh. "Thank you."

"Anytime." Molly smiled.

"I mean she just has no faith. You know?" Ginny looked up at her maid of honor for agreement.

"I know."

"We still have a whole half an hour."

Her friend nodded. "Mm, hm."

"That's plenty of time for him to get here," Ginny continued, trying to believe her own words. Somehow maintaining faith amid the complete lack of proof, of any reassurance that Thom was even on his way.

A knock on the door had her turning, eyes wide.

"That could be him." Ginny grasped the handle and yanked the door open.

She searched the faces of the men in uniform there, looking for *her* man in uniform. She hadn't found him yet as one guy stepped forward, his hand extended.

"Ginny. Good to see you again." As she struggled to come up with a name for the slightly familiar man, he continued, "We met when you were visiting Thom. I'm Grant Milton."

"Of course. Sorry. It's just been one hell of a day already. Nice to see you again." Ginny shook the man's warm hand.

When he released his hold on her, he took a step back to include the rest of the group. "Some of these guys you might know, and some you might not. This is Craig Dawson and James MacIntyre and back there are Will, Clyde, and Fitz. A couple of the guys couldn't make it up from Virginia but they send their best wishes."

His kindness and that all these guys had traveled so far to be here, when she was very aware of how much pulling of military strings that had taken, nearly broke Ginny's tentative hold on her composure. "Thank you all for coming. Um, Thom's not here yet."

Grant's brow furrowed. "Oh. Well, I guess it is bad luck for the groom to see the bride before the wedding so he'll probably get here right before the ceremony."

"That's probably it. We can use all the good luck we can get, right?" She forced a laugh and realized it came out sounding more like a manic giggle. "Thanks again for coming."

"Sure. No problem. I'll let you get back to getting ready now." He smiled.

"Thanks." Ginny held on to her composure until

she closed the door, then she sagged against it, holding in the tears pricking behind her eyes. She refused to show anyone, even Molly, how worried she truly was.

"Oh. My. God. Tell me some of those guys are single. And that you're going to let me visit you down in Virginia."

Luckily for Ginny, Molly's attention had been elsewhere. She'd been too busy ogling the SEALs.

"Of course. You can visit me anytime you want." Ginny only hoped she'd actually be living in Virginia. As the minutes passed, she was beginning to have doubts, in spite of herself.

Molly eyed her closely. "You doing all right?"

"Yeah."

"Can I get you something?"

Some peace and quiet where no one asked her how she was doing. The groom. All things Ginny would love right about now.

"Some water?" Ginny asked instead.

"Sure. Right away. There's a water cooler out in the vestibule. I'll be right back."

Molly rushed out to get the water and Ginny braced her hands against the table in front of the mirror concentrating on breathing when it felt like her chest was too tight to fit her lungs.

Efficient as ever, Molly returned in no time bearing not one but two cups of water and Ginny's peace and quiet came to an end.

"Here you go. I brought two. They're small." Molly put both down on the table next to Ginny's bouquet.

"Thanks." Ginny lifted one little cup and watched the water slosh as her hand trembled.

She took a quick swallow and then put the cup down, reaching instead for her cell phone to check the time.

T-minus-twenty and counting. The vise squeezing her chest got a little bit tighter.

Thom, where are you?

CHAPTER TWENTY-FOUR

"Is that clock right?" Thom asked, because if the time displayed on the dashboard was correct, he had fifteen minutes to get to the church before the ceremony was scheduled to begin.

"I don't know," Rocky said.

"How can you not know?" The question came out sounding a bit too high pitched.

"My cell phone is still hostage in Pennsylvania. And I don't have a watch." Rocky was much too calm.

"I can try to find a station that'll tell us the time." Brody reached for the knob on the radio.

"Never mind." As it was Thom was already teetering on the edge. The noise of the radio would probably push him completely over.

The sign for their upcoming exit whizzed by the

window. "Oh, Thank God. That's our exit."

"I saw. No worries." Rocky steered them from the far left lane to the right.

"We might actually make it on time." Thom started to feel like he could breathe again even as his heart continued to beat too fast.

"Yup. Told you," Brody said as Rocky took the exit ramp and then turned onto the main road.

Thom wasn't going to praise Brody on his prediction because making it to the church with just minutes to spare, and getting married in the clothes he'd been wearing for two days instead of his dress uniform, wasn't anything to be happy about.

But even as crazed as Thom felt—and had felt for the past three hours—he couldn't help but see a glimmer of hope, a light at the end of the dark tunnel as they got closer to the church.

Ginny might be pissed but at least he'd make it. He wouldn't completely miss the wedding—

"Shit. What the fuck is this?" Rocky slammed on the brake pedal as the road in front of them became a sea of stopped cars and glowing red brake lights.

Since they were at a complete standstill, Rocky rolled down the window and shouted to a couple walking on the street, "What's going on up there?"

"Parade," the woman answered.

"Shit." Thom's heart, impossibly, pounded faster. "How close are we?" he asked Brody.

Brody, acting as navigator, referred to the paper printout of the MapQuest directions in his hand.

Good thing Ginny was obsessively compulsive about things at times. He'd told her they'd be fine using their cell phones' GPS and map app but she'd still insisted on printing out the directions to and from the cabin for them. And also had insisted he take a copy of the directions to the church that she'd printed out for everyone they'd invited.

Thank God for Ginny since—as Rocky had said—their phones were no longer in their possession.

"It looks like about half a mile. Straight on this road. The church is on the corner on the right three blocks up."

"I'm going on foot. Let me out of here."

Turning in his seat Rocky shot Thom a look of surprise, but said, "Okay."

Rocky unlocked the door, hopped down and flipped the seat so Thom could crawl out. "I can't leave the truck here—"

Thom waved off Rocky's concern. "I know. Meet you there."

Thom took off at a sprint, dodging pedestrians who were there to watch the parade. Weaving through the middle of the marching band currently blocking the intersection. Ignoring the cop who blew his whistle and then shouted at him for busting through the parade.

He was too close to Ginny, and to making it to this wedding in time, to let anyone stop him now.

The church came into view, its steeple soaring high into the sky above the neighboring buildings. It was like an oasis in the desert and pushed Thom to run faster.

He leapt over the curb, sprinted up the walkway

and took the wide stone stairs two at a time. He was about to yank open the door of the church when he heard his name being called.

Thom spun and saw Chris Cassidy and Grant Milton standing off to the side.

That visual confirmation that he was at the right place at the right time, in combination with his sprint, doubled him over at the waist.

"Oh my God." Hands braced on his knees, Thom was panting hard as Chris and Grant moved to his side.

"What happened?" Grant asked.

He didn't have time to answer that. Thom looked up. "Somebody tell Ginny I'm here. Please."

Grant nodded. "I got it."

He turned and rushed through the doors as Thom continued to blow out big bursts of air. Chris stayed there with him.

"When Grant told me you weren't here yet, I came outside to try and call Brody's cell."

Thom nodded. "We had some trouble."

"No shit." Chris snorted. "My brother and Rocky okay?"

"Yeah. They're right behind me with the truck."

Chris shook his head. "I'm sure there's one hell of a story. Can't wait to hear it."

"Later." Thom lifted the edge of his T-shirt to wipe the sweat from his face and started to realize exactly how bad he looked. "Shit. I don't have my uniform here. It's at—"

Even as he said it, the front door of the church swung open and his parents ran out.

"Oh, thank God." His mother flung herself at him, hugging him in spite of the sweat.

His father stood just behind her. "It's good to see you, son. We were worried."

"I know. Sorry." Eventually he'd have to tell everyone what had happened but as crazy as everything that happened was, it wasn't going to be a quick story. "I need to get inside and, I don't know, try to get cleaned up a little."

The door opened again and Grant emerged and—in a miraculous turn of events—he was carrying a dry cleaning bag containing what looked like Thom's uniform.

"Is that mine?" Thom asked, eyes wide.

Grant grinned. "Sure is. Your very organized bride brought it with her."

"How is she doing?" he asked, afraid to hear the answer.

The wobbling of Grant's head as he grimaced didn't make Thom feel better. "I'm not going to lie to you. There were some tears. Happy tears I hope, but yeah, she's emotional."

Thom didn't blame her. "Okay, I'm going to go find a bathroom, get washed up as best I can, and try to make myself presentable enough to not embarrass this uniform."

Grant handed Thom the hanger. "Need help?"

He would have normally said no, but he was shaking so badly a steady pair of hands helping him wasn't a bad idea. And Grant knew the uniform and the proper way to wear it, which Thom's father, the next best choice to help him, did not.

"I'd appreciate that. Thanks."

With Grant's help, Thom was dressed and ready in minutes. The preacher had checked on him in the men's room and said to take his time, even while glancing at his watch, so Thom didn't delay.

"Someone will tell Ginny we're ready?" Thom asked as he stood in the vestibule with Grant.

Her father was standing nearby, no doubt waiting to walk his only daughter down the aisle.

"I'll tell her." He smiled and Thom had hope the man might not hate him for the rest of his married life for today's debacle.

"Thank you, sir." Thom turned and blew out a breath. "Okay. I guess I'm ready."

Grant nodded and then frowned. "Who's your best man?"

"My dad." Thom glanced toward the altar through the glass window in the vestibule doors. "Looks like he's up there with the preacher, probably trying to smooth over the situation, knowing him."

Grant smiled. "Okay. Well, good luck."

"Thanks." For once, Thom felt like he actually had some good luck.

He strode through the doors and all eyes turned toward him. Yeah, he probably should have asked if there was another way to the altar. He was about to walk up the aisle when two smiling faces stopped him mid-step.

"Jason. Juliette." Thom squatted next to the last pew and hugged each one of his children. His eyes misted and he finally understood Ginny's concept of happy tears. "I didn't know you guys would be here."

"Mom brought us," Juliette answered when her face was no longer buried in Thom's chest.

Thom pulled back from the hug and there was his ex-wife. Last they'd talked, or rather fought, she'd said no to the kids coming, yet here she was.

Forcing a close-lipped smile, she said, "Hey."

"Hey." He stood. "I wasn't expecting you."

She let out a laugh. "I wasn't expecting this either. My mother shamed me into it."

His mother in law, whom he thought had always hated him? That was a surprise.

"Really?" he asked.

"Yup. I was talking to her after I got the invitation with the hand written note saying you two would love if I could attend along with the children."

Thom frowned. "When did that come in the mail?"

"Tuesday. In an Express Mail envelope."

That would have been mailed after he'd gotten to Connecticut and told Ginny how upset he was because the kids wouldn't be there.

He shook his head. "I didn't send that."

"I didn't think you did. It was clearly from Ginny. Anyway, Mom said the kids should be here for you . . . and I realized she was right."

Organ music began to play, reminding Thom he was holding up the wedding when the preacher was already unhappy with him for delaying the start time.

"I, uh, gotta go." He tipped his head toward the altar.

"Yeah." She nodded, looking not at all thrilled to be there, but it didn't matter because his kids were there.

Thom bent quick and kissed each one. "Talk to you two in a little bit."

He strode forward fast to take his place next to his father.

They wasted no time getting started. The moment he turned back to face the aisle he'd just walked down, both doors were swung wide and secured open to reveal Molly, looking very maid of honor-like in her pink dress and bouquet. She walked the aisle at a stately pace and smiled at him when she reached the end, before stepping to the side and turning.

Thom's gaze shot to the doorway and to the woman in white on her father's arm. His woman. Soon, his wife.

She walked a bit faster than Molly had, and he couldn't blame her. He'd made her wait too long already.

Her father kissed her on the cheek, tipped his head to Thom and turned to take his seat next to Ginny's weeping mother in the front pew.

He new mother-in-law wasn't the only one crying. Ginny took one look at him and her eyes filled with tears.

He took both of her hands in his. "Shh. It's okay. Don't cry. I'm here."

She drew in a big shaky breath that broke his

heart as he fully absorbed how badly he'd worried her. "I already cried off my make-up once today. Molly had to fix it."

"You look absolutely beautiful. And I'm so sorry I made you cry."

"It's okay." Ginny sniffed in one more big breath—steadier than the first—and then blew it out slowly through her mouth before she turned toward the preacher. "Okay. Ready to start?"

The preacher nodded, cleared his throat and said, "Dearly beloved . . ."

In his peripheral vision, Thom saw Brody and Rocky sneak into the back of the church.

All hands accounted for.

He smiled and turned his full attention to the preacher and, more importantly, his bride.

CHAPTER TWENTY-FIVE

"Mr. and Mrs. Thomas Grande. Virginia Starr-Grande." Ginny tried the two names out aloud to see how they felt.

Thom cocked one brow high and bobbed his head. "A hyphen. Nice. I like it."

"Really? Because I'm not so sure." Ginny screwed up her mouth in indecision.

Thom broke into a smile. "Baby, I don't care what name you choose to go by as long as you're my wife."

"Aw. You're so sweet." The champagne she'd started drinking at noon had begun to go to her head. She leaned against Thom, happy for more than one reason that his arms were wrapped around her.

"So does that mean I'm forgiven?" he asked.

"Yes. Of course. Jeez." She had to admit the story he'd told her had sounded pretty nuts at first, but seeing Rocky using a cell phone borrowed from Brody's brother to call his family to tell them about what had happened had gone a long way to add legitimacy to the three men's tale.

So had the fact Thom looked as if he hadn't slept all night and was downing water like he hadn't had anything to drink in days.

The guys had also been on the phone with Jon Rudnick, Thom's former teammate who'd left the Navy and opened a private security company, to see what he could dig up with his resources.

Meanwhile, the SEAL she'd been introduced to as Will had whipped a laptop out of his car and was currently camped out on a table on her parents' lawn while surrounded by more SEALs, all looking very serious.

"What's going on over there?" she asked, tipping her chin in their direction.

"Will's tracing our cell phone signals to see if the guys who had us have moved."

"He can do that?" she asked.

"You have no idea." Thom laughed at her obvious surprise before getting serious. He pressed his lips together. "Are you really okay? Are *we* okay? I know I scared the hell out of you and I can't possibly apologize enough for that."

"We're good." She pressed closer feeling playful fueled with champagne and her new-bride happiness. "Very good. I'll prove it to you later, husband."

"I look forward to it." He glanced around them before dipping his head. Holding her chin between his thumb and forefinger, Thom lowered his head and pressed a heated kiss to her lips. When he pulled back he said, "And might I add I'm very happy this thing is going to end early tonight."

"Me too."

"But, eventually, we're going to have to talk seriously about things."

"Things? What things?" Ginny had been too serious for too long now, with Thom's constant deploying, and the wedding plans and then his disappearance. She didn't want to have to be serious again anytime soon.

"For one," he began. "Why did you assure me your mother was okay with you moving when she's not? You should have told me."

She shook her head. "It was my problem to handle, not yours."

"No." He formed the word while shaking his head. "That's not how—"

"*Not how this works. We're a team,*" she talked over him, quoting his words back to him, knowing the sentiment by heart by now. He'd said it at least twice already, maybe more.

Thom pressed his lips together. "It's true."

"I didn't want to worry you before you went away." Ginny had been more concerned about Thom coming back with his team in one piece than about her mother being a little upset she was moving away.

He tilted his head. "Give me some credit, baby.

I'm a little tougher than that."

She lifted her brows. "I could say the same thing to you about me. I can handle this."

Eyes focused on her, he finally tipped his head. "Okay. Duly noted."

"Thank you. And how'd you find out she's unhappy anyway?"

"Besides her icy response by the buffet when Grant mentioned us living in Virginia, you mean?" He laughed. "Your father told my father."

"Really? Hmm." Their fathers were bonding. Interesting. She'd think more about that later. "Now, I have a question for you."

With his warm hands still wrapped around her waist, where she hoped they'd stay for a long time, he said, "Okay, shoot."

"What's with the full moon?" she asked.

"What?" He looked confused.

"You asked me to choose a wedding date near the full moon. Why? I googled my butt off trying to find out what the significance was but I couldn't find anything. Well, actually I found a ton of stuff but nothing that I thought had anything to do with you, so why? I mean this party is basically going to end at sunset, so it's not like we're going to enjoy the moon or anything." As he grinned she frowned. "Please tell me before the curiosity kills me."

He chuckled. "I believe curiosity could kill you. Ginny, really, it's not a big deal."

"Then tell me." She was moments away from stomping her foot in frustration.

"I don't know. Maybe I'll make you suffer—"

"Thom!"

"Okay. Okay." He grinned. "Darkness is a SEAL's best friend. The full moon, not so much. Too bright. So we're less likely to be scheduled for an op then."

"Oh. That's it?" she asked, frowning.

"Yeah. That's it."

"That doesn't sound top secret to me."

He laughed. "It's not."

"Then why didn't you tell me?"

"Because you didn't ask."

Ginny sighed. "I see being married to you is going to be an adventure."

"Right back at you, baby." Thom smiled.

"Oh, I forgot to tell you. I was talking to Debbie and we decided it would be nice if we could all spend Thanksgiving together. You, me, her, the kids. We could even invite your parents down. And mine. We'll be settled in our new place by then."

Thom swallowed hard enough she saw his throat work. "Yeah, sure. That's a, uh, good idea."

"Right? I'm so glad you agree. I thought so too. I'm excited." Ginny smiled, already planning the menu in her head.

"Yeah, uh, me too." He pulled her closer to him and blew out a big sigh and her marital bliss bubbled over.

EPILOGUE

"Hey, bro. Happy Thanksgiving."

At the sound of the familiar voice behind him, Thom turned. "Hey. Happy Thanksgiving to you too."

Rocky smiled. "Look at us. Two married men doing a little grocery shopping at the commissary the day before Thanksgiving."

Thom tossed the bag of groceries Ginny had sent him out to buy into the back of the SUV and turned back to Rocky. "Yup. Looks like we've been domesticated." He laughed.

"Completely," Rocky agreed. "So uh, hey, I heard from my father. It looks like our *friends* in Pennsylvania are going to have a court battle on their hands. He said the DA is looking to throw everything she can at them."

"Good." Thom couldn't say he felt bad about that, considering.

"More and more shit is coming out about the group. Apparently Ray had been a member of the state militia—which is a legal recognized group—but he was a little too extreme in his ideas for them. When they suggested he wasn't a good fit for the group, he went off and started his own."

"The one who took us."

Rocky nodded. "Yup."

That group seemed extreme all right. It all made sense.

"The Pennsylvania State Militia is pretty pissed that Ray's group is giving them a bad reputation so they're happy to testify against him."

"Good. Thanks for the update."

"Sure. So how's things going over at your place?" Rocky's grin told Thom his friend was amused at his expense.

"You mean with my parents and my in-laws there now and my ex-wife and kids all coming tomorrow for Thanksgiving dinner? Yeah, it's just been a ton of fun. Thanks." Thom rolled his eyes, which only had Rocky laughing aloud.

"You're married to one helluva special woman there. She got everyone to agree to spend the day together. I'd say it's the next biggest accomplishment to brokering peace in the Middle East."

"Yeah, I guess so." Thom sighed.

Meanwhile, their house on base was full to overflowing since both sets of parents had arrived that afternoon. One reason why he'd been more than happy to go shopping for the last minute things Ginny needed for tomorrow's dinner.

Rocky shook his head. "Better you than me, man. I'm not sure I'd be able to handle it. I mean the ex-wife and the wife, together. Maybe even becoming friends."

Thom shook his head. "I'm not too worried about it."

Rocky lifted a brow. "You should be. What do you think the topic of conversation is going to be when those two are together tomorrow? You."

"Let's hope you're wrong. I'm just happy to have my kids and my parents with me for the holiday."

It didn't happen often enough he got to be home and with family on a holiday and not off in some other part of the world. Given all that, he had plenty to be thankful for—even with Debbie as his and Ginny's dinner guest.

"All right. I guess I'd better get back. Izzy's waiting on me." Rocky extended his right hand and shook Thom's. "Hey, we'll see you this weekend."

Thom nodded. "You will."

Ginny had orchestrated some gathering for Sunday night after their parents all left for home.

Friendsgiving, she called it. Apparently it was a thing. All the guys who were in town for the weekend and their wives or girlfriends were coming over to his place to eat turkey leftovers. It might actually be fun so he didn't fight her on it.

"Happy Thanksgiving," Rocky said one more

time. "And if you need to escape for a few minutes, or for a few beers, give me a call."

Thom smiled. "I might do that. Thanks."

As Rocky headed for his truck, Thom climbed into the driver's seat of his SUV.

Three quarters of a mile away, he pulled behind his parents' car in the driveway of the house he and Ginny had made a home.

She opened the front door and smiled as he climbed the front stairs, grocery bag in hand. "Hey."

"Hey." He leaned low and kissed her, still not used to her being there to greet him when he arrived home.

Every time he saw her there, he got a thrill. He hoped the feeling never went away.

"Was the store very crowded?" she asked.

"Nope. Not too bad. Not as crowded as our house, anyway." He smiled, closing the door behind him.

Ginny cringed as she took the bag from his hand. "I know. I'm sorry."

"Don't be sorry. I like having the whole family here." And if the surgery he and Ginny had discussed, the one to reverse his vasectomy, was successful, perhaps next Thanksgiving the house would be a little more crowded.

A baby of their own. A little brother or sister for Jason and Juliette. Thom couldn't wait.

He pulled Ginny close. "I love you."

"And I love you." She tipped her head to one side. "Wanna help me make the cranberry sauce while the parents are busy in the living room looking at the wedding album?"

Smiling, he said, "There's nothing I'd like more."

In case you missed it . . .
Read how it all began! You can find the story of
how Thom and Ginny first met in
SEALed at Midnight

Hot SEALs

Night with a SEAL
Saved by a SEAL
SEALed at Midnight
Kissed by a SEAL
Protected by a SEAL
Loved by a SEAL
Tempted by a SEAL
Wed to a SEAL
Romanced by a SEAL
Rescued by a Hot SEAL
Betting on a Hot SEAL
Escape with a Hot SEAL
Matched with a Hot SEAL
SEAL the Deal

For more titles by Cat visit CatJohnson.net

ABOUT THE AUTHOR

Cat Johnson is a top 10 *New York Times* bestseller and the author of the *USA Today* bestselling Hot SEALs series. She writes contemporary romance featuring sexy alpha heroes and is known for her unique marketing. She has sponsored pro bull riders, owns a collection of camouflage and western wear for book signings, and has used bologna to promote romance novels.

Never miss a new release or a sale again. Join Cat's inner circle at catjohnson.net/news.

51295562R00117

Made in the USA
San Bernardino, CA
18 July 2017